Alfred Tennyson

A Selection from the Works of Alfred Tennyson

Alfred Tennyson

A Selection from the Works of Alfred Tennyson

ISBN/EAN: 9783337277369

Printed in Europe, USA, Canada, Australia, Japan

Cover: Foto ©Andreas Hilbeck / pixelio.de

More available books at **www.hansebooks.com**

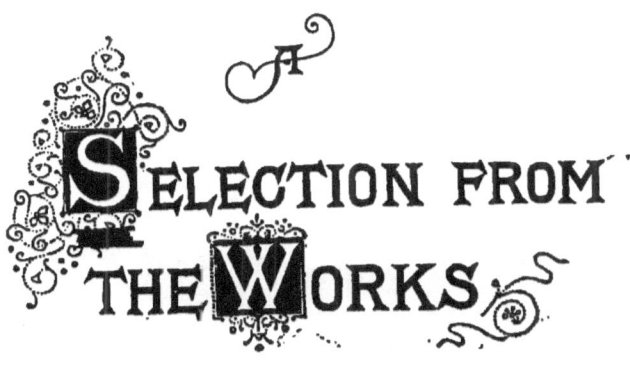

A SELECTION FROM THE WORKS

OF

ALFRED TENNYSON, D.C.L.,

POET LAUREATE.

LONDON:
EDWARD MOXON & CO., DOVER STREET.
1865.

CONTENTS.

	PAGE
TO THE QUEEN	1
THE MAY QUEEN	3
NEW-YEAR'S EVE	7
CONCLUSION	12
THE GRANDMOTHER	17
THE EAGLE	28
GODIVA	29
MARIANA	33
THE CAPTAIN	37
"COME NOT, WHEN I AM DEAD"	40
ST. AGNES' EVE	41
SIR GALAHAD	43
DORA	47
THE MILLER'S DAUGHTER	54
THE LORD OF BURLEIGH	65
LADY CLARE	69
THE LADY OF SHALOTT	73
THE BEGGAR MAID	81
LADY CLARA VERE DE VERE	82

CONTENTS.

	PAGE
THE GARDENER'S DAUGHTER; OR, THE PICTURES	86
LOCKSLEY HALL	97
THE BROOK	117
EDWARD GRAY	127
ŒNONE	129
TITHONUS	141
ULYSSES	145
THE GOLDEN YEAR	148
THE VISION OF SIN	151
MORTE D'ARTHUR	161
ODE ON THE DEATH OF THE DUKE OF WELLINGTON	172
BRITAIN	184
FREEDOM	186
"COME INTO THE GARDEN, MAUD"	188
THE SAILOR BOY	190
"MY LIFE IS FULL OF WEARY DAYS"	191
"BREAK, BREAK, BREAK"	192
THE CHARGE OF THE LIGHT BRIGADE	193
THREE SONNETS TO A COQUETTE	196
"GO NOT, HAPPY DAY"	198
A FAREWELL	199
"AS THRO' THE LAND AT EVE WE WENT"	200
"SWEET AND LOW, SWEET AND LOW"	201
"THE SPLENDOUR FALLS ON CASTLE WALLS"	202
"TEARS, IDLE TEARS, I KNOW NOT WHAT THEY MEAN"	203
"O SWALLOW, SWALLOW, FLYING, FLYING SOUTH"	205
SONG	207
SONG	207

CONTENTS.

PAGE

"HOME THEY BROUGHT HER WARRIOR DEAD" . 208

"ASK ME NO MORE: THE MOON MAY DRAW THE SEA" 209

"NOW SLEEPS THE CRIMSON PETAL, NOW THE WHITE" 210

"COME DOWN, O MAID, FROM YONDER MOUNTAIN

    HEIGHT" 211

CRADLE SONG 213

ENID'S SONG 214

VIVIEN'S SONG 215

ELAINE'S SONG 216

THE DEPARTURE 217

WILL 219

ON A MOURNER 220

THE SEA-FAIRIES 222

THE POET'S SONG 224

GUINEVERE 225

DEDICATION. OF THE "IDYLLS OF THE KING" . . 254

TO THE QUEEN.

REVERED, beloved—O you that hold
  A nobler office upon earth
  Than arms, or power of brain, or birth
Could give the warrior kings of old,

VICTORIA,—since your Royal grace
  To one of less desert allows
  This laurel greener from the brows
Of him that utter'd nothing base;

And should your greatness, and the care
  That yokes with empire, yield you time
  To make demand of modern rhyme
If aught of ancient worth be there;

Then—while a sweeter music wakes,
  And thro' wild March the throstle calls,
  Where all about your palace-walls
The sun-lit almond-blossom shakes—

Take, Madam, this poor book of song;
    For tho' the faults were thick as dust
    In vacant chambers, I could trust
Your kindness.   May you rule us long,

And leave us rulers of your blood
    As noble till the latest day!
    May children of our children say,
'She wrought her people lasting good;

'Her court was pure; her life serene;
    God gave her peace; her land reposed;
    A thousand claims to reverence closed
In her as Mother, Wife, and Queen;

'And statesmen at her council met
    Who knew the seasons when to take
    Occasion by the hand, and make
The bounds of freedom wider yet

'By shaping some august decree,
    Which kept her throne unshaken still,
    Broad-based upon her people's will,
And compass'd by the inviolate sea.'

MARCH, 1851.

THE MAY QUEEN.

You must wake and call me early, call me early, mother
    dear;
To-morrow 'll be the happiest time of all the glad New-
    year;
Of all the glad New-year, mother, the maddest merriest
    day;
For I'm to be Queen o' the May, mother, I'm to be
    Queen o' the May.

There's many a black black eye, they say, but none so
    bright as mine;
There's Margaret and Mary, there's Kate and Caroline:
But none so fair as little Alice in all the land they say,
So I'm to be Queen o' the May, mother, I'm to be
    Queen o' the May.

I sleep so sound all night, mother, that I shall never
  wake,
If you do not call me loud when the day begins to break:
But I must gather knots of flowers, and buds and
  garlands gay,
For I'm to be Queen o' the May, mother, I'm to be
  Queen o' the May.

As I came up the valley whom think ye should I see,
But Robin leaning on the bridge beneath the hazel-tree ?
He thought of that sharp look, mother, I gave him
  yesterday,—
But I'm to be Queen o' the May, mother, I'm to be
  Queen o' the May.

He thought I was a ghost, mother, for I was all in white,
And I ran by him without speaking, like a flash of
  light.
They call me cruel-hearted, but I care not what they
  say,
For I'm to be Queen o' the May, mother, I'm to be
  Queen o' the May.

They say he's dying all for love, but that can never be :
They say his heart is breaking, mother—what is that
  to me ?

There's many a bolder lad 'ill woo me any summer day,
And I'm to be Queen o' the May, mother, I'm to be
Queen o' the May.

Little Effie shall go with me to-morrow to the
green,
And you'll be there, too, mother, to see me made the
Queen;
For the shepherd lads on every side 'ill come from far
away,
And I'm to be Queen o' the May, mother, I'm to be
Queen o' the May.

The honeysuckle round the porch has wov'n its wavy
bowers,
And by the meadow-trenches blow the faint sweet
cuckoo-flowers;
And the wild marsh-marigold shines like fire in swamps
and hollows gray,
And I'm to be Queen o' the May, mother, I'm to be
Queen o' the May.

The night-winds come and go, mother, upon the
meadow-grass,
And the happy stars above them seem to brighten as
they pass;

There will not be a drop of rain the whole of the live-
  long day,
And I'm to be Queen o' the May, mother, I'm to be
  Queen o' the May.

All the valley, mother, 'ill be fresh and green and still,
And the cowslip and the crowfoot are over all the hill,
And the rivulet in the flowery dale 'ill merrily glance
  and play,
For I'm to be Queen o' the May, mother, I'm to be
  Queen o' the May.

So you must wake and call me early, call me early,
  mother dear,
To-morrow 'ill be the happiest time of all the glad
  New-year:
To-morrow 'ill be of all the year the maddest merriest
  day,
For I'm to be Queen o' the May, mother, I'm to be
  Queen o' the May.

NEW-YEAR'S EVE.

IF you're waking call me early, call me early, mother
    dear,
For I would see the sun rise upon the glad New-
    year.
It is the last New-year that I shall ever see,
Then you may lay me low i' the mould and think no
    more of me.

To-night I saw the sun set: he set and left behind
The good old year, the dear old time, and all my peace
    of mind;
And the New-year's coming up, mother, but I shall
    never see
The blossom on the blackthorn, the leaf upon the tree.

Last May we made a crown of flowers: we had a
    merry day;
Beneath the hawthorn on the green they made me
    Queen of May;

And we danced about the may-pole and in the hazel-
  copse,
Till Charles's Wain came out above the tall white
  chimney-tops.

There's not a flower on all the hills : the frost is on
  the pane :
I only wish to live till the snowdrops come again :
I wish the snow would melt and the sun come out on
  high :
I long to see a flower so before the day I die.

The building rook 'ill caw from the windy tall elm-tree.
And the tufted plover pipe along the fallow lea,
And the swallow 'ill come back again with summer o'er
  the wave,
But I shall lie alone, mother, within the mouldering
  grave.

Upon the chancel-casement, and upon that grave of
  mine,
In the early early morning the summer sun 'ill shine,
Before the red cock crows from the farm upon the
  hill,
When you are warm-asleep, mother, and all the world
  is still.

When the flowers come again, mother, beneath the
    waning light
You'll never see me more in the long gray fields at
    night;
When from the dry dark wold the summer airs blow
    cool
On the oat-grass and the sword-grass, and the bulrush
    in the pool.

You'll bury me, my mother, just beneath the hawthorn
    shade,
And you'll come sometimes and see me where I am
    lowly laid.
I shall not forget you, mother, I shall hear you when
    you pass,
With your feet above my head in the long and pleasant
    grass.

I have been wild and wayward, but you'll forgive me
    now;
You'll kiss me, my own mother, and forgive me ere
    I go;
Nay, nay, you must not weep, nor let your grief be
    wild,
You should not fret for me, mother, you have another
    child.

If I can I'll come again, mother, from out my resting-
    place;
Tho' you'll not see me, mother, I shall look upon
    your face;
Tho' I cannot speak a word, I shall harken what you
    say,
And be often, often with you when you think I'm far
    away.

Goodnight, goodnight, when I have said goodnight for
    evermore,
And you see me carried out from the threshold of the
    door;
Don't let Effie come to see me till my grave be
    growing green :
She'll be a better child to you than ever I have
    been.

She'll find my garden-tools upon the granary
    floor:
Let her take 'em: they are hers: I shall never garden
    more:
But tell her, when I'm gone, to train the rose-bush
    that I set
About the parlour-window and the box of migno-
    nette.

Good-night, sweet mother: call me before the day is
    born.
All night I lay awake, but I fall asleep at morn;
But I would see the sun rise upon the glad New-year,
So, if you're waking, call me, call me early, mother dear.

CONCLUSION.

I THOUGHT to pass away before, and yet alive I am;
And in the fields all round I hear the bleating of the
     lamb.
How sadly, I remember, rose the morning of the year!
To die before the snowdrop came, and now the violet's
     here.

O sweet is the new violet, that comes beneath the
     skies,
And sweeter is the young lamb's voice to me that
     cannot rise,
And sweet is all the land about, and all the flowers
     that blow,
And sweeter far is death than life to me that long to go.

It seem'd so hard at first, mother, to leave the blessed
     sun,
And now it seems as hard to stay, and yet His will be
     done !

But still I think it can't be long before I find release;
And that good man, the clergyman, has told me words
    of peace.

O blessings on his kindly voice and on his silver
    hair !
And blessings on his whole life long, until he meet me
    there !
O blessings on his kindly heart and on his silver
    head !
A thousand times I blest him, as he knelt beside my
    bed.

He taught me all the mercy, for he show'd me all the sin.
Now, tho' my lamp was lighted late, there's One will
    let me in:
Nor would I now be well, mother, again if that could be,
For my desire is but to pass to Him that died for me.

I did not hear the dog howl, mother, or the death-
    watch beat,
There came a sweeter token when the night and
    morning meet:
But sit beside my bed, mother, and put your hand in
    mine,
And Effie on the other side, and I will tell the sign.

All in the wild March-morning I heard the angels
        call;
It was when the moon was setting, and the dark was
        over all;
The trees began to whisper, and the wind began to
        roll,
And in the wild March-morning I heard them call my
        soul.

For lying broad awake I thought of you and Effie dear;
I saw you sitting in the house, and I no longer here;
With all my strength I pray'd for both, and so I felt
        resign'd,
And up the valley came a swell of music on the wind.

I thought that it was fancy, and I listen'd in my bed,
And then did something speak to me—I know not
        what was said;
For great delight and shuddering took hold of all my
        mind,
And up the valley came again the music on the wind.

But you were sleeping; and I said, "It's not for them:
        it's mine."
And if it comes three times, I thought, I take it for
        a sign.

And once again it came, and close beside the window-
    bars,
Then seem'd to go right up to Heaven and die among
    the stars.

So now I think my time is near. I trust it is. I
    know
The blessed music went that way my soul will have
    to go.
And for myself, indeed, I care not if I go to-day.
But, Effie, you must comfort *her* when I am past
    away.

And say to Robin a kind word, and tell him not to
    fret ;
There's many worthier than I, would make him happy
    yet.
If I had lived—I cannot tell—I might have been his
    wife;
But all these things have ceased to be, with my desire
    of life.

O look! the sun begins to rise, the heavens are in a
    glow;
He shines upon a hundred fields, and all of them I
    know.

And there I move no longer now, and there his light
     may shine—
Wild flowers in the valley for other hands than mine.

O sweet and strange it seems to me, that ere this day
     is done
The voice, that now is speaking, may be beyond the
     sun—
For ever and for ever with those just souls and true—
And what is life, that we should moan? why make we
     such ado?

For ever and for ever, all in a blessed home—
And there to wait a little while till you and Effie
     come—
To lie within the light of God, as I lie upon your
     breast—
And the wicked cease from troubling, and the weary
     are at rest.

THE GRANDMOTHER.

I.

AND Willy, my eldest-born, is gone, you say, little
   Anne?
Ruddy and white, and strong on his legs, he looks like
   a man.
And Willy's wife has written: she never was over-
   wise,
Never the wife for Willy: he wouldn't take my
   advice.

II.

For, Annie, you see, her father was not the man to
   save,
Hadn't a head to manage, and drank himself into his
   grave.

C

Pretty enough, very pretty! but I was against it for
    one.
Eh!—but he wouldn't hear me—and Willy, you say,
    is gone.

III.

Willy, my beauty, my eldest-born, the flower of the
    flock;
Never a man could fling him: for Willy stood like a
    rock.
' Here's a leg for a babe of a week!' says doctor;
    and he would be bound,
There was not his like that year in twenty parishes
    round.

IV.

Strong of his hands, and strong on his legs, but still of
    his tongue!
I ought to have gone before him: I wonder he went
    so young.
I cannot cry for him, Annie: I have not long to
    stay;
Perhaps I shall see him the sooner, for he lived far
    away.

V.

Why do you look at me, Annie? you think I am hard
  and cold;
But all my children have gone before me, I am so
  old:
I cannot weep for Willy, nor can I weep for the
  rest;
Only at your age, Annie, I could have wept with the
  best.

VI.

For I remember a quarrel I had with your father, my
  dear,
All for a slanderous story, that cost me many a
  tear.
I mean your grandfather, Annie: it cost me a world
  of woe,
Seventy years ago, my darling, seventy years
  ago.

VII.

For Jenny, my cousin, had come to the place, and I
  knew right well .
That Jenny had tript in her time: I knew, but I
  would not tell.

C 2

And she to be coming and slandering me, the base
     little liar !
But the tongue is a fire as you know, my dear, the
     tongue is a fire.

VIII.

And the parson made it his text that week, and he
     said likewise,
That a lie which is half a truth is ever the blackest of
     lies,
That a lie which is all a lie may be met and fought
     with outright,
But a lie which is part a truth is a harder matter to
     fight.

IX.

And Willy had not been down to the farm for a week
     and a day;
And all things look'd half-dead, tho' it was the middle
     of May.
Jenny, to slander me, who knew what Jenny had
     been !
But soiling another, Annie, will never make oneself
     clean.

X.

And I cried myself well-nigh blind, and all of an
evening late
I climb'd to the top of the garth, and stood by the
road at the gate.
The moon like a rick on fire was rising over the
dale,
And whit, whit, whit, in the bush beside me, chirrupt
the nightingale.

XL

All of a sudden he stopt: there past by the gate of
the farm,
Willy,—he didn't see me,—and Jenny hung on his
arm.
Out into the road I started, and spoke I scarce knew
how;
Ah, there's no fool like the old one—it makes me
angry now.

XII.

Willy stood up like a man, and look'd the thing that
he meant;
Jenny, the viper, made me a mocking courtsey and
went.

And I said, 'Let us part: in a hundred years it'll all
    be the same,
You cannot love me at all, if you love not my good
    name.'

            .

XIII.

And he turn'd, and I saw his eyes all wet, in the sweet
    moonshine:
'Sweetheart, I love you so well that your good name
    is mine.
And what do I care for Jane, let her speak of you well
    or ill;
But marry me out of hand: we two shall be happy
    still.'

XIV.

'Marry you, Willy!' said I, 'but I needs must speak
    my mind,
And I fear you'll listen to tales, be jealous and hard
    and unkind.'
But he turn'd and claspt me in his arms, and answer'd,
    'No, love, no;'
Seventy years ago, my darling, seventy years
    ago.

XV.

So Willy and I were wedded : I wore a lilac
    gown ;
And the ringers rang with a will, and he gave the
    ringers a crown.
But the first that ever I bare was dead before he was
    born,
Shadow and shine is life, little Annie, flower and
    thorn.

XVI.

That was the first time, too, that ever I thought of
    death.
There lay the sweet little body that never had drawn
    a breath.
I had not wept, little Anne, not since I had been a
    wife;
But I wept like a child that day, for the babe had
    fought for his life.

XVII.

His dear little face was troubled, as if with anger or
    pain:
I look'd at the still little body—his trouble had all
    been in vain.

For Willy I cannot weep, I shall see him another
　　morn:
But I wept like a child for the child that was dead
　　before he was born.

XVIII.

But he cheer'd me, my good man, for he seldom said
　　me nay:
Kind, like a man, was he; like a man, too, would
　　have his way:
Never jealous—not he: we had many a happy
　　year;
And he died, and I could not weep—my own time
　　seem'd so near.

XIX.

But I wish'd it had been God's will that I, too, then
　　could have died:
I began to be tired a little, and fain had slept at his
　　side.
And that was ten years back, or more, if I don't
　　forget:
But as to the children, Annie, they're all about me
　　yet.

XX.

Pattering over the boards, my Annie who left me
    at two,
Patter she goes, my own little Annie, an Annie like
    you:
Pattering over the boards, she comes and goes at
    her will,
While Harry is in the five-acre and Charlie ploughing
    the hill.

XXI.

And Harry and Charlie, I hear them too—they sing
    to their team:
Often they come to the door in a pleasant kind of a
    dream.
They come and sit by my chair,-they hover about
    my bed—
I am not always certain if they be alive or
    dead.

XXII.

And yet I know for a truth, there's none of them
    left alive;
For Harry went at sixty, your father at sixty-
    five:

And Willy, my eldest born, at nigh threescore and
　　ten;
I knew them all as babies, and now they're elderly
　　men.

XXIII.

For mine is a time of peace, it is not often I
　　grieve;
I am oftener sitting at home in my father's farm
　　at eve:
And the neighbours come and laugh and gossip, and
　　so do I;
I find myself often laughing at things that have long
　　gone by.

XXIV.

To be sure the preacher says, our sins should make
　　us sad:
But mine is a time of peace, and there is Grace to
　　be had;
And God, not man, is the Judge of us all when life
　　shall cease;
And in this Book, little Annie, the message is one of
　　Peace.

XXV.

And age is a time of peace, so it be free from
pain,
And happy has been my life; but I would not live
it again.
I seem to be tired a little, that's all, and long for
rest;
Only at your age, Annie, I could have wept with the
best.

XXVI.

So Willy has gone, my beauty, my eldest-born, my
flower;
But how can I weep for Willy, he has but gone for
an hour,—
Gone for a minute, my son, from this room into the
next;
I, too, shall go in a minute. What time have I to
be vext?

XXVII.

And Willy's wife has written, she never was over-
wise.
Get me my glasses, Annie: thank God that I keep
my eyes.

There is but a trifle left you, when I shall have past
   away.
But stay with the old woman now: you cannot have
   long to stay.

THE EAGLE.

He clasps the crag with crooked hands;
Close to the sun in lonely lands,
Ring'd with the azure world, he stands.

The wrinkled sea beneath him crawls;
He watches from his mountain walls,
And like a thunderbolt he falls.

GODIVA.

I waited for the train at Coventry;
I hung with grooms and porters on the bridge,
To watch the three tall spires; and there I shaped
The city's ancient legend into this :—
　　Not only we, the latest seed of Time,
New men, that in the flying of a wheel
Cry down the past, not only we, that prate
Of rights and wrongs, have loved the people well,
And loathed to see them overtax'd; but she
Did more, and underwent, and overcame,
The woman of a thousand summers back,
Godiva, wife to that grim Earl, who ruled
In Coventry: for when he laid a tax
Upon his town, and all the mothers brought
Their children, clamouring, "If we pay, we starve!"
She sought her lord, and found him, where he strode
About the hall, among his dogs, alone,

His beard a foot before him, and his hair
A yard behind.   She told him of their tears,
And pray'd him, " If they pay this tax, they starve."
Whereat he stared, replying, half-amazed,
" You would not let your little finger ache
For such as *these?*"—" But I would die," said she.
He laugh'd, and swore by Peter and by Paul:
Then fillip'd at the diamond in her ear;
" O ay, ay, ay, you talk!"—"Alas!" she said,
" But prove me what it is I would not do."
And from a heart as rough as Esau's hand,   ·
He answer'd, " Ride you naked thro' the town,
And I repeal it;" and nodding, as in scorn,
He parted, with great strides among his dogs.
   So left alone, the passions of her mind,
As winds from all the compass shift and blow,
Made war upon each other for an hour,
Till pity won.   She sent a herald forth,
And bade him cry, with sound of trumpet, all
The hard condition; but that she would loose
The people: therefore, as they loved her well,
From then till noon no foot should pace the street,
No eye look down, she passing; but that all
Should keep within, door shut, and window barr'd.
   Then fled she to her inmost bower, and there
Unclasp'd the wedded eagles of her belt,

The grim Earl's gift; but ever at a breath
She linger'd, looking like a summer moon
Half-dipt in cloud: anon she shook her head,
And shower'd the rippled ringlets to her knee;
Unclad herself in haste; adown the stair
Stole on; and, like a creeping sunbeam, slid
From pillar unto pillar, until she reach'd
The gateway; there she found her palfrey trapt
In purple blazon'd with armorial gold.
　　Then she rode forth, clothed on with chastity:
The deep air listen'd round her as she rode,
And all the low wind hardly breathed for fear.
The little wide-mouth'd heads upon the spout
Had cunning eyes to see: the barking cur
Made her cheek flame: her palfrey's footfall shot
Light horrors thro' her pulses: the blind walls
Were full of chinks and holes; and overhead
Fantastic gables, crowding, stared: but she
Not less thro' all bore up, till, last, she saw
The white-flower'd elder-thicket from the field
Gleam thro' the Gothic archways in the wall.
　　Then she rode back, clothed on with chastity:
And one low churl, compact of thankless earth,
The fatal byword of all years to come,
Boring a little augur-hole in fear,
Peep'd—but his eyes, before they had their will,

Were shrivell'd into darkness in his head,
And dropt before him.   So the Powers, who wait
On noble deeds, cancell'd a sense misused;
And she, that knew not, pass'd: and all at once,
With twelve great shocks of sound, the shameless noon
Was clash'd and hammer'd from a hundred towers,
One after one: but even then she gain'd
Her bower; whence reissuing, robed and crown'd.
To meet her lord, she took the tax away,
And built herself an everlasting name.

MARIANA.

"Mariana in the moated grange."—Measure for Measure.

WITH blackest moss the flower-plots
    Were thickly crusted, one and all:
The rusted nails fell from the knots
    That held the pear to the garden-wall.
The broken sheds look'd sad and strange:
    Unlifted was the clinking latch;
    Weeded and worn the ancient thatch
Upon the lonely moated grange.
       She only said, " My life is dreary,
         He cometh not," she said;
       She said, " I am aweary, aweary,
         I would that I were dead !"

Her tears fell with the dews at even;
    Her tears fell ere the dews were dried;
She could not look on the sweet heaven,
    Either at morn or eventide.

D

After the flitting of the bats,
　When thickest dark did trance the sky,
　She drew her casement-curtain by,
And glanced athwart the glooming flats.
　　She only said, " The night is dreary,
　　　He cometh not," she said;
　　She said, " I am aweary, aweary,
　　　I would that I were dead !"

Upon the middle of the night,
　Waking she heard the night-fowl crow:
The cock sung out an hour ere light:
　From the dark fen the oxen's low
Came to her: without hope of change,
　In sleep she seem'd to walk forlorn,
　Till cold winds woke the gray-eyed morn
About the lonely moated grange.
　　She only said, " The day is dreary,
　　　He cometh not," she said;
　　She said, " I am aweary, aweary,
　　　I would that I were dead !"

About a stone-cast from the wall
　A sluice with blacken'd waters slept,
And o'er it many, round and small,
　The cluster'd marish-mosses crept.

Hard by a poplar shook alway,
 All silver-green with gnarled bark:
 For leagues no other tree did mark
The level waste, the rounding gray.
  She only said, " My life is dreary,
   He cometh not," she said;
  She said, " I am aweary, aweary,
   I would that I were dead !"

And ever when the moon was low,
 And the shrill winds were up and away,
In the white curtain, to and fro,
 She saw the gusty shadow sway.
But when the moon was very low,
 And wild winds bound within their cell,
 The shadow of the poplar fell
Upon her bed, across her brow.
  She only said, " The night is dreary,
   He cometh not," she said;
  She said, " I am aweary, aweary,
   I would that I were dead !"

All day within the dreamy house,
 The doors upon their hinges creak'd;
The blue fly sung in the pane; the mouse
 Behind the mouldering wainscot shriek'd,

Or from the crevice peer'd about.
   Old faces glimmer'd thro' the doors,
   Old footsteps trod the upper floors,
Old voices called her from without.
      She only said, " My life is dreary,
         He cometh not," she said;
      She said, " I am aweary, aweary,
         I would that I were dead !"

The sparrow's chirrup on the roof,
   The slow clock ticking, and the sound
Which to the wooing wind aloof
   The poplar made, did all confound
Her sense; but most she loathed the hour
   When the thick-moted sunbeam lay
   Athwart the chambers, and the day
Was sloping toward his western bower.
      Then, said she, " I am very dreary,
         He will not come," she said;
      She wept, " I am aweary, aweary,
         Oh God, that I were dead !"

THE CAPTAIN.

A LEGEND OF THE NAVY.

HE that only rules by terror
 Doeth grievous wrong.
Deep as Hell I count his error.
 Let him hear my song.
Brave the Captain was: the seamen
 Made a gallant crew,
Gallant sons of English freemen,
 Sailors bold and true.
But they hated his oppression,
 Stern he was and rash;
So for every light transgression
 Doom'd them to the lash.
Day by day more harsh and cruel
 Seem'd the Captain's mood.
Secret wrath like smother'd fuel
 Burnt in each man's blood.
Yet he hoped to purchase glory,
 Hoped to make the name
Of his vessel great in story,
 Wheresoe'er he came.

So they past by capes and islands,
   Many a harbour-mouth,
Sailing under palmy highlands
   Far within the South.
On a day when they were going
   O'er the lone expanse,
In the north, her canvas flowing,
   Rose a ship of France.
Then the Captain's colour heighten'd,
   Joyful came his speech:
But a cloudy gladness lighten'd
   In the eyes of each.
" Chase," he said: the ship flew forward,
   And the wind did blow;
Stately, lightly, went she Norward,
   Till she near'd the foe.
Then they look'd at him they hated,
   . Had what they desired:
Mute with folded arms they waited—
   ˙ Not a gun was fired.
But they heard the foeman's thunder
   Roaring out their doom;
All the air was torn in sunder,
   Crashing went the boom,
Spars were splinter'd, decks were shatter'd,
   Bullets fell like rain;

Over mast and deck were scatter'd
  Blood and brains of men.
Spars were splinter'd; decks were broken:
  Every mother's son—
Down they dropt—no word was spoken—
  Each beside his gun.
On the decks as they were lying,
  Were their faces grim.
In their blood, as they lay dying,
  Did they smile on him.
Those, in whom he had reliance
  For his noble name,
With one smile of still defiance
  Sold him unto shame.
Shame and wrath his heart confounded,
  Pale he turn'd and red,
Till himself was deadly wounded
  Falling on the dead.
Dismal error! fearful slaughter!
  Years have wander'd by,
Side by side beneath the water
  Crew and Captain lie;
There the sunlit ocean tosses
  O'er them mouldering,
And the lonely seabird crosses
  With one waft of the wing.

Come not, when I am dead,
　To drop thy foolish tears upon my grave,
To trample round my fallen head,
　And vex the unhappy dust thou wouldst not save.
There let the wind sweep and the plover cry;
　　　But thou, go by.

Child, if it were thine error or thy crime
　I care no longer, being all unblest:
Wed whom thou wilt, but I am sick of Time,
　And I desire to rest.
Pass on, weak heart, and leave me where I lie:
　　Go by, go by.

ST. AGNES' EVE.

DEEP on the convent-roof the snows
  Are sparkling to the moon:
My breath to heaven like vapour goes:
  May my soul follow soon!
The shadows of the convent-towers
  Slant down the snowy sward,
Still creeping with the creeping hours
  That lead me to my Lord:
Make Thou my spirit pure and clear
  As are the frosty skies,
Or this first snowdrop of the year
  That in my bosom lies.

As these white robes are soil'd and dark,
  To yonder shining ground;
As this pale taper's earthly spark,
  To yonder argent round;

So shows my soul before the Lamb,
    My spirit before Thee;
So in mine earthly house I am,
    To that I hope to be.
Break up the heavens, O Lord! and far,
    Thro' all yon starlight keen,
Draw me, thy bride, a glittering star,
    In raiment white and clean.

He lifts me to the golden doors;
    The flashes come and go;
All heaven bursts her starry floors,
    And strows her lights below,
And deepens on and up! the gates
    Roll back, and far within
For me the Heavenly Bridegroom waits,
    To make me pure of sin.
The sabbaths of Eternity,
    One sabbath deep and wide—
A light upon the shining sea—
    The Bridegroom with his bride!

SIR GALAHAD.

My good blade carves the casques of men,
　My tough lance thrusteth sure,
My strength is as the strength of ten,
　Because my heart is pure.
The shattering trumpet shrilleth high,
　The hard brands shiver on the steel,
The splinter'd spear-shafts crack and fly,
　The horse and rider reel:
They reel, they roll in clanging lists,
　And when the tide of combat stands,
Perfume and flowers fall in showers,
　That lightly rain from ladies' hands.

How sweet are looks that ladies bend
　On whom their favours fall!
For them I battle till the end,
　To save from shame and thrall:

But all my heart is drawn above,
    My knees are bow'd in crypt and shrine:
I never felt the kiss of love,
    Nor maiden's hand in mine.
More bounteous aspects on me beam,
    Me mightier transports move and thrill;
So keep I fair thro' faith and prayer
    A virgin heart in work and will.

When down the stormy crescent goes,
    A light before me swims,
Between dark stems the forest glows,
    I hear a noise of hymns:
Then by some secret shrine I ride;
    I hear a voice, but none are there;
The stalls are void, the doors are wide,
    The tapers burning fair.
Fair gleams the snowy altar-cloth,
    The silver vessels sparkle clean,
The shrill bell rings, the censer swings,
    And solemn chaunts resound between.

Sometimes on lonely mountain-meres
    I find a magic bark;
I leap on board: no helmsman steers:
    I float till all is dark.

A gentle sound, an awful light!
   Three angels bear the holy Grail:
With folded feet, in stoles of white,
   On sleeping wings they sail.
Ah, blessed vision! blood of God!
   My spirit beats her mortal bars,
As down dark tides the glory slides,
   And star-like mingles with the stars.

When on my goodly charger borne
   Thro' dreaming towns I go,
The cock crows ere the Christmas morn,
   The streets are dumb with snow.
The tempest crackles on the leads,
   And, ringing, springs from brand and mail;
But o'er the dark a glory spreads,
   And gilds the driving hail.
I leave the plain, I climb the height;
   No branchy thicket shelter yields;
But blessed forms in whistling storms
   Fly o'er waste fens and windy fields.

A maiden knight—to me is given
   Such hope, I know not fear;
I yearn to breathe the airs of heaven
   That often meet me here.

I muse on joy that will not cease,
   Pure spaces clothed in living beams,
Pure lilies of eternal peace,
   Whose odours haunt my dreams;
And, stricken by an angel's hand,
   This mortal armour that I wear,
This weight and size, this heart and eyes,
   Are touch'd, are turn'd to finest air.

The clouds are broken in the sky,
   And thro' the mountain-walls
A rolling organ-harmony
   Swells up, and shakes and falls.
Then move the trees, the copses nod,
   Wings flutter, voices hover clear:
"O just and faithful knight of God!
   Ride on! the prize is near."
So pass I hostel, hall, and grange;
   By bridge and ford, by park and pale,
All-arm'd I ride, whate'er betide,
   Until I find the holy Grail.

DORA.

WITH farmer Allan at the farm abode
William and Dora. William was his son,
And she his niece. He often look'd at them,
And often thought " I'll make them man and wife."
Now Dora felt her uncle's will in all,
And yearn'd towards William; but the youth, because
He had been always with her in the house,
Thought not of Dora.
     Then there came a day
When Allan call'd his son, and said, " My son:
I married late, but I would wish to see
My grandchild on my knees before I die:
And I have set my heart upon a match.
Now therefore look to Dora; she is well
To look to; thrifty too beyond her age.
She is my brother's daughter: he and I
Had once hard words, and parted, and he died
In foreign lands; but for his sake I bred .
His daughter Dora: take her for your wife;

For I have wish'd this marriage, night and day,
For many years." But William answer'd short;
"I cannot marry Dora; by my life,
I will not marry Dora." Then the old man
Was wroth, and doubled up his hands, and said:
"You will not, boy! you dare to answer thus!
But in my time a father's word was law,
And so it shall be now for me. Look to it;
Consider, William: take a month to think,
And let me have an answer to my wish;
Or, by the Lord that made me, you shall pack,
And never more darken my doors again."
But William answer'd madly; bit his lips,
And broke away. The more he look'd at her
The less he liked her; and his ways were harsh;
But Dora bore them meekly. Then before
The month was out he left his father's house,
And hired himself to work within the fields;
And half in love, half spite, he woo'd and wed
A labourer's daughter, Mary Morrison.

    Then, when the bells were ringing, Allan call'd
His niece and said: "My girl, I love you well;
But if you speak with him that was my son,
Or change a word with her he calls his wife,
My home is none of yours. My will is law."
And Dora promised, being meek. She thought,

"It cannot be: my uncle's mind will change!"
And days went on, and there was born a boy
To William; then distresses came on him;
And day by day he pass'd his father's gate,
Heart-broken, and his father help'd him not.
But Dora stored what little she could save,
And sent it them by stealth, nor did they know
Who sent it; till at last a fever seized
On William, and in harvest time he died.
Then Dora went to Mary. Mary sat
And look'd with tears upon her boy, and thought
Hard things of Dora. Dora came and said:
"I have obey'd my uncle until now,
And I have sinn'd, for it was all thro' me
This evil came on William at the first.
But, Mary, for the sake of him that's gone,
And for your sake, the woman that he chose,
And for this orphan, I am come to you:
You know there has not been for these five years
So full a harvest: let me take the boy,
And I will set him in my uncle's eye
Among the wheat; that when his heart is glad
Of the full harvest, he may see the boy,
And bless him for the sake of him that's gone."
And Dora took the child, and went her way
Across the wheat, and sat upon a mound

E

That was unsown, where many poppies grew.
Far off the farmer came into the field
And spied her not; for none of all his men
Dare tell him Dora waited with the child;
And Dora would have risen and gone to him,
But her heart fail'd her; and the reapers reap'd,
And the sun fell, and all the land was dark.
But when the morrow came, she rose and took
The child once more, and sat upon the mound;
And made a little wreath of all the flowers
That grew about, and tied it round his hat
To make him pleasing in her uncle's eye.
Then when the farmer pass'd into the field
He spied her, and he left his men at work,
And came and said; "Where were you yesterday?
Whose child is that! What are you doing here?"
So Dora cast her eyes upon the ground,
And answer'd softly, "This is William's child!"
"And did I not," said Allan, "did I not
Forbid you, Dora?" Dora said again;
"Do with me as you will, but take the child
And bless him for the sake of him that's gone!"
And Allan said, "I see it is a trick
Got up betwixt you and the woman there.
I must be taught my duty, and by you!
You knew my word was law, and yet you dared

To slight it. Well—for I will take the boy;
But go you hence, and never see me more."
    So saying, he took the boy, that cried aloud
And struggled hard. The wreath of flowers fell
At Dora's feet. She bow'd upon her hands,
And the boy's cry came to her from the field,
More and more distant. She bow'd down her head,
Remembering the day when first she came,
And all the things that had been. She bow'd down
And wept in secret; and the reapers reap'd,
And the sun fell, and all the land was dark.
    Then Dora went to Mary's house, and stood
Upon the threshold. Mary saw the boy
Was not with Dora. She broke out in praise
To God, that help'd her in her widowhood.
And Dora said, " My uncle took the boy;
But, Mary, let me live and work with you :
He says that he will never see me more."
Then answer'd Mary, " This shall never be,
That thou shouldst take my trouble on thyself :
And, now I think, he shall not have the boy,
For he will teach him hardness, and to slight
His mother; therefore thou and I will go,
And I will have my boy, and bring him home;
And I will beg of him to take thee back :
But if he will not take thee back again,

Then thou and I will live within one house,
And work for William's child, until he grows
Of age to help us."

                So the women kiss'd
Each other, and set out, and reach'd the farm.
The door was off the latch : they peep'd, and saw
The boy set up betwixt his grandsire's knees,
Who thrust him in the hollows of his arm,
And clapt him on the hands and on the cheeks,
Like one that loved him : and the lad stretch'd out
And babbled for the golden seal, that hung
From Allan's watch, and sparkled by the fire.
Then they came in : but when the boy beheld
His mother, he cried out to come to her :
And Allan set him down, and Mary said :

    " O Father !—if you let me call you so—
I never came a-begging for myself,
Or William, or this child ; but now I come
For Dora : take her back ; she loves you well.
O Sir, when William died, he died at peace
With all men ; for I ask'd him, and he said,
He could not ever rue his marrying me—
I had been a patient wife : but, Sir, he said
That he was wrong to cross his father thus :
' God bless him !' he said, ' and may he never know
The troubles I have gone thro' !' Then he turn'd

His face and pass'd—unhappy that I am !
But now, Sir, let me have my boy, for you
Will make him hard, and he will learn to slight
His father's memory; and take Dora back,
And let all this be as it was before."
 So Mary said, and Dora hid her face
By Mary. There was silence in the room;
And all at once the old man burst in sobs :—
  " I have been to blame—to blame. I have kill'd
      my son.
I have kill'd him—but I loved him—my dear son.
May God forgive me !—I have been to blame.
Kiss me, my children."
                    Then they clung about
The old man's neck, and kiss'd him many times.
And all the man was broken with remorse ;
And all his love came back a hundredfold ;
And for three hours he sobb'd o'er William's child,
Thinking of William.
                    So those four abode
Within one house together; and as years
Went forward, Mary took another mate ;
But Dora lived unmarried till her death.

THE MILLER'S DAUGHTER.

I SEE the wealthy miller yet,
  His double chin, his portly size,
And who that knew him could forget
  The busy wrinkles round his eyes?
The slow wise smile that, round about
  His dusty forehead drily curl'd,
Seem'd half-within and half-without,
  And full of dealings with the world?

In yonder chair I see him sit,
  Three fingers round the old silver cup—
I see his gray eyes twinkle yet
  At his own jest—gray eyes lit up
With summer lightnings of a soul
  So full of summer warmth, so glad,
So healthy, sound, and clear and whole,
  His memory scarce can make me sad.

Yet fill my glass: give me one kiss:
    My own sweet Alice, we must die.
There's somewhat in this world amiss
    Shall be unriddled by and by.
There's somewhat flows to us in life,
    But more is taken quite away.
Pray, Alice, pray, my darling wife,
    That we may die the self-same day.

Have I not found a happy earth?
    I least should breathe a thought of pain.
Would God renew me from my birth
    I'd almost live my life again.
So sweet it seems with thee to walk,
    And once again to woo thee mine—
It seems in after-dinner talk
    Across the walnuts and the wine—

To be the long and listless boy
    Late-left an orphan of the squire,
Where this old mansion mounted high
    Looks down upon the village spire:
For even here, where I and you
    Have lived and loved alone so long,
Each morn my sleep was broken thro'
    By some wild skylark's matin song.

And oft I heard the tender dove
  In firry woodlands making moan ;
But ere I saw your eyes, my love,
  I had no motion of my own.
For scarce my life with fancy play'd
  Before I dream'd that pleasant dream—
Still hither thither idly sway'd
  Like those long mosses in the stream.

Or from the bridge I lean'd to hear
  The milldam rushing down with noise,
And see the minnows everywhere
  In crystal eddies glance and poise,
The tall flag-flowers when they sprung
  Below the range of stepping-stones,
Or those three chestnuts near, that hung
  In masses thick with milky cones.

But, Alice, what an hour was that,
  When after roving in the woods
('Twas April then), I came and sat
  Below the chestnuts, when their buds
Were glistening to the breezy blue ;
  And on the slope, an absent fool,
I cast me down, nor thought of you,
  But angled in the higher pool.

A love-song I had somewhere read,
  An echo from a measured strain,
Beat time to nothing in my head
  From some odd corner of the brain.
It haunted me, the morning long,
  With weary sameness in the rhymes,
The phantom of a silent song,
  That went and came a thousand times.

Then leapt a trout.   In lazy mood
  I watch'd the little circles die ;
They past into the level flood,
  And there a vision caught my eye ;
The reflex of a beauteous form,
  A glowing arm, a gleaming neck,
As when a sunbeam wavers warm
  Within the dark and dimpled beck.

For you remember, you had set,
  That morning, on the casement's edge
A long green box of mignonette,
  And you were leaning from the ledge :
And when I raised my eyes, above
  They met with two so full and bright—
Such eyes !   I swear to you, my love,
  That these have never lost their light.

I loved, and love dispell'd the fear
   That I should die an early death :
For love possess'd the atmosphere,
   And fill'd the breast with purer breath.
My mother thought, What ails the boy?
   For I was alter'd, and began
To move about the house with joy,
   And with the certain step of man.

I loved the brimming wave that swam
   Thro' quiet meadows round the mill,
The sleepy pool above the dam,
   The pool beneath it never still,
The meal-sacks on the whiten'd floor,
   The dark round of the dripping wheel,
The very air about the door
   Made misty with the floating meal.

And oft in ramblings on the wold,
   When April nights began to blow,
And April's crescent glimmer'd cold,
   I saw the village lights below;
I knew your taper far away,
   And full at heart of trembling hope,
From off the wold I came, and lay
   Upon the freshly-flower'd slope.

The deep brook groan'd beneath the mill;
 And " by that lamp," I thought, " she sits !"
The white chalk-quarry from the hill
 Gleam'd to the flying moon by fits.
" O that I were beside her now !
 O will she answer if I call?
O would she give me vow for vow,
 Sweet Alice, if I told her all?"

Sometimes I saw you sit and spin;
 And, in the pauses of the wind,
Sometimes I heard you sing within;
 Sometimes your shadow cross'd the blind.
At last you rose and moved the light,
 And the long shadow of the chair
Flitted across into the night,
 And all the casement darken'd there.

But when at last I dared to speak,
 The lanes, you know, were white with may,
Your ripe lips moved not, but your cheek
 Flush'd like the coming of the day;
And so it was—half-sly, half-shy,
 You would, and would not, little one !
Although I pleaded tenderly,
 And you and I were all alone.

And slowly was my mother brought
    To yield consent to my desire :
She wish'd me happy, but she thought
    I might have look'd a little higher;
And I was young—too young to wed :
    " Yet must I love her for your sake ;
Go fetch your Alice here," she said :
    Her eyelid quiver'd as she spake.

And down I went to fetch my bride :
    But, Alice, you were ill at ease ;
This dress and that by turns you tried,
    Too fearful that you should not please.
I loved you better for your fears,
    I knew you could not look but well ;
And dews, that would have fall'n in tears,
    I kiss'd away before they fell.

I watch'd the little flutterings,
    The doubt my mother would not see ;
She spoke at large of many things,
    And at the last she spoke of me ;
And turning look'd upon your face,
    As near this door you sat apart,
And rose, and, with a silent grace
    Approaching, press'd you heart to heart.

Ah, well—but sing the foolish song
  I gave you, Alice, on the day
When, arm in arm, we went along,
  A pensive pair, and you were gay
With bridal flowers—that I may seem,
  As in the nights of old, to lie
Beside the mill-wheel in the stream,
  While those full chestnuts whisper by.

It is the miller's daughter,
  And she is grown so dear, so dear,
That I would be the jewel
  That trembles at her ear:
For hid in ringlets day and night,
I'd touch her neck so warm and white.

And I would be the girdle
  About her dainty dainty waist,
And her heart would beat against me,
  In sorrow and in rest :
And I should know if it beat right,
I'd clasp it round so close and tight.

And I would be the necklace,
  And all day long to fall and rise
Upon her balmy bosom,
  With her laughter or her sighs,
And I would lie so light, so light,
I scarce should be unclasp'd at night.

A trifle, sweet! which true love spells—
    True love interprets—right alone.
His light upon the letter dwells,
    For all the spirit is his own.
So, if I waste words now, in truth
    You must blame Love.   His early rage
Had force to make me rhyme in youth,
    And makes me talk too much in age.

And now those vivid hours are gone,
    Like mine own life to me thou art,
Where Past and Present, wound in one,
    Do make a garland for the heart:
So sing that other song I made,
    Half-anger'd with my happy lot,
The day, when in the chestnut shade
    I found the blue Forget-me-not.

Love that hath us in the net,
Can he pass, and we forget?
Many suns arise and set.
Many a chance the years beget.
Love the gift is Love the debt.
    Even so.
Love is hurt with jar and fret.
Love is made a vague regret.

Eyes with idle tears are wet.
Idle habit links us yet.
What is love? for we forget:
    Ah, no! no!

Look thro' mine eyes with thine. True wife,
  Round my true heart thine arms entwine;
My other dearer life in life,
  Look thro' my very soul with thine!
Untouch'd with any shade of years,
  May those kind eyes for ever dwell!
They have not shed a many tears,
  Dear eyes, since first I knew them well.

Yet tears they shed: they had their part
  Of sorrow: for when time was ripe,
The still affection of the heart
  Became an outward breathing type,
That into stillness past again,
  And left a want unknown before;
Although the loss that brought us pain,
  That loss but made us love the more,

With farther lookings on. The kiss,
  The woven arms, seem but to be

Weak symbols of the settled bliss,
    The comfort, I have found in thee:
But that God bless thee, dear—who wrought
    Two spirits to one equal mind—
With blessings beyond hope or thought,
    With blessings which no words can find.

Arise, and let us wander forth,
    To yon old mill across the wolds;
For look, the sunset, south and north,
    Winds all the vale in rosy folds,
And fires your narrow casement glass,
    Touching the sullen pool below:
On the chalk-hill the bearded grass
    Is dry and dewless.   Let us go.

THE LORD OF BURLEIGH.

In her ear he whispers gaily,
  "If my heart by signs can tell,
Maiden, I have watch'd thee daily,
  And I think thou lov'st me well."
She replies, in accents fainter,
  "There is none I love like thee."
He is but a landscape-painter,
  And a village maiden she.
He to lips, that fondly falter,
  Presses his without reproof:
Leads her to the village altar,
  And they leave her father's roof.
"I can make no marriage present:
  Little can I give my wife.
Love will make our cottage pleasant,
  And I love thee more than life."
They by parks and lodges going
  See the lordly castles stand:
Summer woods, about them blowing,
  Made a murmur in the land.
From deep thought himself he rouses,
  Says to her that loves him well,

F

"Let us see these handsome houses
   Where the wealthy nobles dwell."
So she goes by him attended,
   Hears him lovingly converse,
Sees whatever fair and splendid
   Lay betwixt his home and hers;
Parks with oak and chestnut shady,
   Parks and order'd gardens great,
Ancient homes of lord and lady,
   Built for pleasure and for state.
All he shows her makes him dearer:
   Evermore she seems to gaze
On that cottage growing nearer,
   Where they twain will spend their days.
O but she will love him truly!
   He shall have a cheerful home;
She will order all things duly,
   When beneath his roof they come.
Thus her heart rejoices greatly,
   Till a gateway she discerns
With armorial bearings stately,
   And beneath the gate she turns;
Sees a mansion more majestic
   Than all those she saw before:
Many a gallant gay domestic
   Bows before him at the door.

And they speak in gentle murmur,
    When they answer to his call,
While he treads with footstep firmer,
    Leading on from hall to hall.
And, while now she wonders blindly,
    Nor the meaning can divine,
Proudly turns he round and kindly,
    "All of this is mine and thine."
Here he lives in state and bounty,
    Lord of Burleigh, fair and free,
Not a lord in all the county
    Is so great a lord as he.
All at once the colour flushes
    Her sweet face from brow to chin:
As it were with shame she blushes,
    And her spirit changed within.
Then her countenance all over
    Pale again as death did prove:
But he clasp'd her like a lover,
    And he cheer'd her soul with love.
So she strove against her weakness,
    Tho' at times her spirit sank:
Shaped her heart with woman's meekness
    To all duties of her rank:
And a gentle consort made he,
    And her gentle mind was such

F 2

That she grew a noble lady,
　　And the people loved her much.
But a trouble weigh'd upon her,
　　And perplex'd her, night and morn,
With the burthen of an honour
　　Unto which she was not born.
Faint she grew, and ever fainter,
　　And she murmur'd, " Oh, that he
Were once more that landscape-painter,
　　Which did win my heart from me!"
So she droop'd and droop'd before him,
　　Fading slowly from his side:
Three fair children first she bore him,
　　Then before her time she died.
Weeping, weeping late and early,
　　Walking up and pacing down,
Deeply mourn'd the Lord of Burleigh,
　　Burleigh-house by Stamford-town.
And he came to look upon her,
　　And he look'd at her and said,
" Bring the dress and put it on her,
　　That she wore when she was wed."
Then her people, softly treading,
　　Bore to earth her body, drest
In the dress that she was wed in,
　　That her spirit might have rest.

LADY CLARE.

IT was the time when lilies blow,
  And clouds are highest up in air,
Lord Ronald brought a lily-white doe
  To give his cousin, Lady Clare.

I trow they did not part in scorn:
  Lovers long-betroth'd were they:
They two will wed the morrow morn:
  God's blessing on the day!

"He does not love me for my birth,
  Nor for my lands so broad and fair;
He loves me for my own true worth,
  And that is well," said Lady Clare.

In there came old Alice the nurse,
  Said, "Who was this that went from thee?"
"It was my cousin," said Lady Clare,
  "To-morrow he weds with me."

"O God be thank'd!" said Alice the nurse,
  "That all comes round so just and fair:
Lord Ronald is heir of all your lands,
  And you are not the Lady Clare."

" Are ye out of your mind, my nurse, my nurse ?"
    Said Lady Clare, " that ye speak so wild ?"
" As God's above," said Alice the nurse,
    " I speak the truth: you are my child.

" The old Earl's daughter died at my breast;
    I speak the truth, as I live by bread !
I buried her like my own sweet child,
    And put my child in her stead."

" Falsely, falsely have ye done,
    O mother," she said, " if this be true,
To keep the best man under the sun
    So many years from his due."

" Nay now, my child," said Alice the nurse,
    " But keep the secret for your life,
And all you have will be Lord Ronald's,
    When you are man and wife."

" If I'm a beggar born," she said,
    " I will speak out, for I dare not lie.
Pull off, pull off, the broach of gold,
    And fling the diamond necklace by."

" Nay now, my child," said Alice the nurse,
    " But keep the secret all ye can."
She said " Not so: but I will know
    If there be any faith in man."

" Nay now, what faith ? " said Alice the nurse,
   " The man will cleave unto his right."
" And he shall have it," the lady replied,
   " Tho' I should die to-night."

"Yet give one kiss to your mother dear !
   Alas, my child, I sinn'd for thee."
" O mother, mother, mother," she said,
   " So strange it seems to me.

" Yet here's a kiss for my mother dear,
   My mother dear, if this be so,
And lay your hand upon my head,
   And bless me, mother, ere I go."

She clad herself in a russet gown,
   She was no longer Lady Clare:
She went by dale, and she went by down,
   With a single rose in her hair.

The lily-white doe Lord Ronald had brought
   Leapt up from where she lay,
Dropt her head in the maiden's hand,
   And follow'd her all the way.

Down stept Lord Ronald from his tower:
   "O Lady Clare, you shame your worth !
Why come you drest like a village maid,
   That are the flower of the earth ? "

" If I come drest like a village maid,
  I am but as my fortunes are :
I am a beggar born," she said,
  " And not the Lady Clare."

" Play me no tricks," said Lord Ronald,
  " For I am yours in word and in deed.
Play me no tricks," said Lord Ronald,
  " Your riddle is hard to read."

O and proudly stood she up !
  Her heart within her did not fail :
She look'd into Lord Ronald's eyes,
  And told him all her nurse's tale.

He laugh'd a laugh of merry scorn :
  He turn'd and kiss'd her where she stood :
" If you are not the heiress born,
  And I," said he, " the next in blood—

" If you are not the heiress born,
  And I," said he, " the lawful heir,
We two will wed to-morrow morn,
  And you shall still be Lady Clare."

THE LADY OF SHALOTT.

PART I.

On either 'side the river lie
Long fields of barley and of rye,
That clothe the wold and meet the sky;
And thro' the field the road runs by
            To many-tower'd Camelot;
And up and down the people go,
Gazing where the lilies blow
Round an island there below,
            The island of Shalott.

Willows whiten, aspens quiver,
Little breezes dusk and shiver
Thro' the wave that runs for ever
By the island in the river
            Flowing down to Camelot.

Four gray walls, and four gray towers,
Overlook a space of flowers,
And the silent isle imbowers
      The Lady of Shalott.

By the margin, willow-veil'd,
Slide the heavy barges trail'd
By slow horses; and unhail'd
The shallop flitteth silken-sail'd
      Skimming down to Camelot:
But who hath seen her wave her hand ?
Or at the casement seen her stand ?
Or is she known in all the land,
      The Lady of Shalott ?

Only reapers, reaping early
In among the bearded barley,
Hear a song that echoes cheerly
From the river winding clearly,
      Down to tower'd Camelot:
And by the moon the reaper weary,
Piling sheaves in uplands airy,
Listening, whispers " 'Tis the fairy
      Lady of Shalott."

PART II.

THERE she weaves by night and day
A magic web with colours gay.
She has heard a whisper say,
A curse is on her if she stay
   To look down to Camelot.
She knows not what the curse may be,
And so she weaveth steadily, ·
And little other care hath she,
   The Lady of Shalott.

And moving thro' a mirror clear
That hangs before her all the year,
Shadows of the world appear.
There she sees the highway near
   Winding down to Camelot:
There the river eddy whirls,
And there the surly village-churls,
And the red cloaks of market girls,
   Pass onward from Shalott.

Sometimes a troop of damsels glad,
An abbot on an ambling pad,
Sometimes a curly shepherd-lad,
Or long-hair'd page in crimson clad,
   Goes by to tower'd Camelot;

And sometimes thro' the mirror blue
The knights come riding two and two:
She hath no loyal knight and true,
       The Lady of Shalott.

But in her web she still delights
To weave the mirror's magic sights,
For often thro' the silent nights
A funeral, with plumes and lights,
       And music, went to Camelot:
Or when the moon was overhead,
Came two young lovers lately wed;
" I am half sick of shadows," said
       The Lady of Shalott.

PART III.

A BOW-SHOT from her bower-eaves,
He rode between the barley-sheaves,
The sun came dazzling thro' the leaves,
And flamed upon the brazen greaves
       Of bold Sir Lancelot.
A red-cross knight for ever kneel'd
To a lady in his shield,
That sparkled on the yellow field,
       Beside remote Shalott.

The gemmy bridle glitter'd free,
Like to some branch of stars we see
Hung in the golden Galaxy.
The bridle bells rang merrily
        As he rode down to Camelot:
And from his blazon'd baldric slung
A mighty silver bugle hung,
And as he rode his armour rung,
        Beside remote Shalott.

All in the blue unclouded weather
Thick-jewell'd shone the saddle-leather,
The helmet and the helmet-feather
Burn'd like one burning flame together,
        As he rode down to Camelot.
As often thro' the purple night,
Below the starry clusters bright,
Some bearded meteor, trailing light,
        Moves over still Shalott.

His broad clear brow in sunlight glow'd;
On burnish'd hooves his war-horse trode;
From underneath his helmet flow'd
His coal-black curls as on he rode,
        As he rode down to Camelot.

From the bank and from the river
He flash'd into the crystal mirror,
" Tirra lirra," by the river
    Sang Sir Lancelot.

She left the web, she left the loom,
She made three paces thro' the room,
She saw the water-lily bloom,
She saw the helmet and the plume,
    She look'd down to Camelot.
Out flew the web and floated wide;
The mirror crack'd from side to side;
" The curse is come upon me," cried
    The Lady of Shalott.

PART IV.

In the stormy east-wind straining,
The pale yellow woods were waning,
The broad stream in his banks complaining,
Heavily the low sky raining
    Over tower'd Camelot;
Down she came and found a boat
Beneath a willow left afloat,
And round about the prow she wrote
    The Lady of Shalott.

And down the river's dim expanse—
Like some bold seër in a trance,
Seeing all his own mischance—
With a glassy countenance
      Did she look to Camelot.
And at the closing of the day
She loosed the chain, and down she lay;
The broad stream bore her far away,
      The Lady of Shalott.

Lying, robed in snowy white
That loosely flew to left and right—
The leaves upon her falling light—
Thro' the noises of the night
      She floated down to Camelot:
And as the boat-head wound along
The willowy hills and fields among,
They heard her singing her last song,
      The Lady of Shalott.

Heard a carol, mournful, holy,
Chanted loudly, chanted lowly,
Till her blood was frozen slowly,
And her eyes were darken'd wholly,
      Turn'd to tower'd Camelot.

For ere she reach'd upon the tide
The first house by the water-side,
Singing in her song she died,
      The Lady of Shalott.

Under tower and balcony,
By garden-wall and gallery,
A gleaming shape she floated by,
Dead-pale between the houses high,
      Silent into Camelot.
Out upon the wharfs they came,
Knight and burgher, lord and dame,
And round the prow they read her name,
      The Lady of Shalott.

Who is this? and what is here?
And in the lighted palace near
Died the sound of royal cheer;
And they cross'd themselves for fear,
      All the knights at Camelot:
But Lancelot mused a little space;
He said, " She has a lovely face;
God in his mercy lend her grace,
      The Lady of Shalott."

THE BEGGAR MAID.

HER arms across her breast she laid;
   She was more fair than words can say:
Bare-footed came the beggar maid
   Before the king Cophetua.
In robe and crown the king stept down,
   To meet and greet her on her way;
"It is no wonder," said the lords,
   "She is more beautiful than day."

As shines the moon in clouded skies,
   She in her poor attire was seen:
One praised her ancles, one her eyes,
   One her dark hair and lovesome mien.
So sweet a face, such angel grace,
   In all that land had never been:
Cophetua sware a royal oath:
   "This beggar maid shall be my queen !"

G

LADY CLARA VERE DE VERE.

LADY Clara Vere de Vere,
  Of me you shall not win renown:
You thought to break a country heart
  For pastime, ere you went to town.
At me you smiled, but unbeguiled
  I saw the snare, and I retired:
The daughter of a hundred Earls,
  You are not one to be desired.

Lady Clara Vere de Vere,
  I know you proud to bear your name,
Your pride is yet no mate for mine,
  Too proud to care from whence I came.
Nor would I break for your sweet sake
  A heart that doats on truer charms.
A simple maiden in her flower
  Is worth a hundred coats-of-arms.

Lady Clara Vere de Vere,
   Some meeker pupil you must find,
For were you queen of all that is,
   I could not stoop to such a mind.
You sought to prove how I could love,
   And my disdain is my reply.
The lion on your old stone gates
   Is not more cold to you than I.

Lady Clara Vere de Vere,
   You put strange memories in my head.
Not thrice your branching limes have blown
   Since I beheld young Laurence dead.
Oh your sweet eyes, your low replies:
   A great enchantress you may be;
But there was that across his throat
   Which you had hardly cared to see.

Lady Clara Vere de Vere,
   When thus he met his mother's view,
She had the passions of her kind,
   She spake some certain truths of you.
Indeed I heard one bitter word
   That scarce is fit for you to hear;
Her manners had not that repose
   Which stamps the caste of Vere de Vere.

Lady Clara Vere de Vere,
    There stands a spectre in your hall:
The guilt of blood is at your door:
    You changed a wholesome heart to gall.
You held your course without remorse,
    To make him trust his modest worth,
And, last, you fix'd a vacant stare,
    And slew him with your noble birth.

Trust me, Clara Vere de Vere,
    From yon blue heavens above us bent
The grand old gardener and his wife
    Smile at the claims of long descent.
Howe'er it be, it seems to me,
    'Tis only noble to be good.
Kind hearts are more than coronets,
    And simple faith than Norman blood.

I know you, Clara Vere de Vere:
    You pine among your halls and towers:
The languid light of your proud eyes
    Is wearied of the rolling hours.
In glowing health, with boundless wealth,
    But sickening of a vague disease,
You know so ill to deal with time,
    You needs must play such pranks as these.

Clara, Clara Vere de Vere,
   If Time be heavy on your hands,
Are there no beggars at your gate,
   Nor any poor about your lands?
Oh ! teach the orphan-boy to read,
   Or teach the orphan-girl to sew,
Pray Heaven for a human heart,
   And let the foolish yeoman go.

THE GARDENER'S DAUGHTER;

Or, THE PICTURES.

THIS morning is the morning of the day,
When I and Eustace from the city went
To see the Gardener's Daughter; I and he,
Brothers in Art; a friendship so complete
Portion'd in halves between us, that we grew
The fable of the city where we dwelt.

    My Eustace might have sat for Hercules;
So muscular he spread, so broad of breast.
He, by some law that holds in love, and draws
The greater to the lesser, long desired
A certain miracle of symmetry,
A miniature of loveliness, all grace
Summ'd up and closed in little;—Juliet, she
So light of foot, so light of spirit—oh, she
To me myself, for some three careless moons,
The summer pilot of an empty heart
Unto the shores of nothing! Know you not
Such touches are but embassies of love,
To tamper with the feelings, ere he found

Empire for life? but Eustace painted her,
And said to me, she sitting with us then,
"When will *you* paint like this?" and I replied,
(My words were half in earnest, half in jest,)
" 'Tis not your work, but Love's.   Love, unperceived,
A more ideal Artist he than all,
Came, drew your pencil from you, made those eyes
Darker than darkest pansies, and that hair
More black than ashbuds in the front of March."
And Juliet answer'd laughing, "Go and see
The Gardener's daughter: trust me, after that,
You scarce can fail to match his masterpiece."
And up we rose, and on the spur we went.

   Not wholly in the busy world, nor quite
Beyond it, blooms the garden that I love.
News from the humming city comes to it
In sound of funeral or of marriage bells;
And, sitting muffled in dark leaves, you hear
The windy clanging of the minster clock;
Although between it and the garden lies
A league of grass, wash'd by a slow broad stream,
That, stirr'd with languid pulses of the oar,
Waves all its lazy lilies, and creeps on,
Barge-laden, to three arches of a bridge
Crown'd with the minster-towers.

                 The fields between

Are dewy-fresh, browsed by deep-udder'd kine,
And all about the large lime feathers low,
The lime a summer home of murmurous wings.

In that still place she, hoarded in herself,
Grew, seldom seen: not less among us lived
Her fame from lip to lip. Who had not heard
Of Rose, the Gardener's daughter? Where was he,
So blunt in memory, so old at heart,
At such a distance from his youth in grief,
That, having seen, forgot? The common mouth,
So gross to express delight, in praise of her
Grew oratory. Such a lord is Love,
And Beauty such a mistress of the world.

And if I said that Fancy, led by Love,
Would play with flying forms and images,
Yet this is also true, that, long before
I look'd upon her, when I heard her name
My heart was like a prophet to my heart,
And told me I should love. A crowd of hopes,
That sought to sow themselves like winged seeds,
Born out of everything I heard and saw,
Flutter'd about my senses and my soul;
And vague desires, like fitful blasts of balm
To one that travels quickly, made the air
Of Life delicious, and all kinds of thought,
That verged upon them, sweeter than the dream

Dream'd by a happy man, when the dark East,
Unseen, is brightening to his bridal morn.
    And sure this orbit of the memory folds
For ever in itself the day we went
To see her.   All the land in flowery squares,
Beneath a broad and equal-blowing wind,
Smelt of the coming summer, as one large cloud
Drew downward: but all else of Heaven was pure
Up to the Sun, and May from verge to verge,
And May with me from head to heel.   And now,
As tho' 'twere yesterday, as tho' it were
The hour just flown, that morn with all its sound,
(For those old Mays had thrice the life of these,)
Rings in mine ears.   The steer forgot to graze,
And, where the hedge-row cuts the pathway, stood,
Leaning his horns into the neighbour field,
And lowing to his fellows.   From the woods
Came voices of the well-contented doves.
The lark could scarce get out his notes for joy,
But shook his song together as he near'd
His happy home, the ground.   To left and right,
The cuckoo told his name to all the hills;
The mellow ouzel fluted in the elm;
The redcap whistled; and the nightingale
Sang loud, as tho' he were the bird of day.
    And Eustace turn'd, and smiling said to me,

"Hear how the bushes echo! by my life,
These birds have joyful thoughts. Think you they sing
Like poets, from the vanity of song?
Or have they any sense of why they sing?
And would they praise the heavens for what they have?"
And I made answer, "Were there nothing else
For which to praise the heavens but only love,
That only love were cause enough for praise." ·

    Lightly he laugh'd, as one that read my thought,
And on we went; but ere an hour had pass'd,
We reach'd a meadow slanting to the North;
Down which a well-worn pathway courted us
To one green wicket in a privet hedge;
This, yielding, gave into a grassy walk
Thro' crowded lilac-ambush trimly pruned;
And one warm gust, full-fed with perfume, blew
Beyond us, as we enter'd in the cool.
The garden stretches southward. In the midst
A cedar spread his dark-green layers of shade.
The garden-glasses shone, and momently
The twinkling laurel scatter'd silver lights.

    "Eustace," I said, "This wonder keeps the house."
He nodded, but a moment afterwards
He cried, "Look! look!" Before he ceased I turn'd,
And, ere a star can wink, beheld her there.

    For up the porch there grew an Eastern rose,

That, flowering high, the last night's gale had caught,
And blown across the walk.   One arm aloft—
Gown'd in pure white, that fitted to the shape—
Holding the bush, to fix it back, she stood.
A single stream of all her soft brown hair
Pour'd on one side: the shadow of the flowers
Stole all the golden gloss, and, wavering
Lovingly lower, trembled on her waist—
Ah, happy shade—and still went wavering down,
But, ere it touch'd a foot, that might have danced
The greensward into greener circles, dipt,
And mix'd with shadows of the common ground !
But the full day dwelt on her brows, and sunn'd
Her violet eyes, and all her Hebe bloom,
And doubled his own warmth against her lips,
And on the bounteous wave of such a breast
As never pencil drew.   Half light, half shade,
She stood, a sight to make an old man young.
    So rapt, we near'd the house; but she, a Rose
In roses, mingled with her fragrant toil,
Nor heard us come, nor from her tendance turn'd
Into the world without; till close at hand,
And almost ere I knew mine own intent,
This murmur broke the stillness of that air
Which brooded round about her:
                              "Ah, one rose,

One rose, but one, by those fair fingers cull'd,
Were worth a hundred kisses press'd on lips
Less exquisite than thine."
                           She look'd: but all
Suffused with blushes—neither self-possess'd
Nor startled, but betwixt this mood and that,
Divided in a graceful quiet—paused,
And dropt the branch she held, and turning, wound
Her looser hair in braid, and stirr'd her lips
For some sweet answer, tho' no answer came,
Nor yet refused the rose, but granted it,
And moved away, and left me, statue-like,
In act to render thanks.
                           I, that whole day,
Saw her no more, altho' I linger'd there
Till every daisy slept, and Love's white star
Beam'd thro' the thicken'd cedar in the dusk.   .

   So home we went, and all the livelong way
With solemn gibe did Eustace banter me.
"Now," said he, "will you climb the top of Art.
You cannot fail but work in hues to dim
The Titianic Flora. Will you match
My Juliet? you, not you,—the Master, Love,
A more ideal Artist he than all."

   So home I went, but could not sleep for joy,
Reading her perfect features in the gloom,

Kissing the rose she gave me o'er and o'er,
And shaping faithful record of the glance
That graced the giving—such a noise of life
Swarm'd in the golden present, such a voice
Call'd to me from the years to come, and such
A length of bright horizon rimm'd the dark.
And all that night I heard the watchman peal
The sliding season: all that night I heard
The heavy clocks knolling the drowsy hours.
The drowsy hours, dispensers of all good,
O'er the mute city stole with folded wings,
Distilling odours on me as they went
To greet their fairer sisters of the East.

   Love at first sight, first-born, and heir to all,
Made this night thus.   Henceforward squall nor storm
Could keep me from that Eden where she dwelt.
Light pretexts drew me: sometimes a Dutch love
For tulips; then for roses, moss or musk,
To grace my city-rooms; or fruits and cream
Served in the weeping elm; and more and more
A word could bring the colour to my cheek;
A thought would fill my eyes with happy dew;
Love trebled life within me, and with each
The year increased.

              The daughters of the year,
One after one, thro' that still garden pass'd:

Each garlanded with her peculiar flower
Danced into light, and died into the shade;
And each in passing touch'd with some new grace
Or seem'd to touch her, so that day by day,
Like one that never can be wholly known,
Her beauty grew; till Autumn brought an hour
For Eustace, when I heard his deep "I will,"
Breathed, like the covenant of a God, to hold
From thence thro' all the worlds: but I rose up
Full of his bliss, and following her dark eyes
Felt earth as air beneath me, till I reach'd
The wicket-gate, and found her standing there.

There sat we down upon a garden mound,
Two mutually enfolded; Love, the third,
Between us, in the circle of his arms
Enwound us both; and over many a range
Of waning lime the gray cathedral towers,
Across a hazy glimmer of the west,
Reveal'd their shining windows: from them clash'd
The bells; we listen'd; with the time we play'd;
We spoke of other things; we coursed about
The subject most at heart, more near and near,
Like doves about a dovecote, wheeling round
The central wish, until we settled there.

Then, in that time and place, I spoke to her,
Requiring, tho' I knew it was mine own,

Yet for the pleasure that I took to hear,
Requiring at her hand the greatest gift,
A woman's heart, the heart of her I loved;
And in that time and place she answer'd me,
And in the compass of three little words,
More musical than ever came in one,
The silver fragments of a broken voice,
Made me most happy, faltering " I am thine."
  Shall I cease here? Is this enough to say
That my desire, like all strongest hopes,
By its own energy fulfill'd itself,
Merged in completion? Would you learn at full
How passion rose thro' circumstantial grades
Beyond all grades develop'd? and indeed
I had not staid so long to tell you all,
But while I mused came Memory with sad eyes,
Holding the folded annals of my youth;
And while I mused, Love with knit brows went by,
And with a flying finger swept my lips,
And spake, " Be wise: not easily forgiven
Are those, who setting wide the doors, that bar
The secret bridal chambers of the heart,
Let in the day." Here, then, my words have end.
  Yet might I tell of meetings, of farewells—
Of that which came between, more sweet than each,
In whispers, like the whispers of the leaves

That tremble round a nightingale—in sighs
Which perfect Joy, perplex'd for utterance,
Stole from her sister Sorrow.   Might I not tell
Of difference, reconcilement, pledges given,
And vows, where there was never need of vows,
And kisses, where the heart on one wild leap
Hung tranced from all pulsation, as above
The heavens between their fairy fleeces pale
Sow'd all their mystic gulfs with fleeting stars;
Or while the balmy glooming, crescent-lit,
Spread the light haze along the river-shores,
And in the hollows; or as once we met
Unheedful, tho' beneath a whispering rain
Night slid down one long stream of sighing wind,
And in her bosom bore the baby, Sleep.
    But this whole hour your eyes have been intent
On that veil'd picture—veil'd, for what it holds
May not be dwelt on by the common day.
This prelude has prepared thee.   Raise thy soul;
Make thine heart ready with thine eyes: the time
Is come to raise the veil.
                    Behold her there,
As I beheld her ere she knew my heart,
My first, last love; the idol of my youth,
The darling of my manhood, and, alas!
Now the most blessed memory of mine age.

LOCKSLEY HALL.

COMRADES, leave me here a little, while as yet 'tis
    early morn:
Leave me here, and when you want me, sound upon
    the bugle horn.

'Tis the place, and all around it, as of old, the curlews
    call,
Dreary gleams about the moorland flying over Locksley
    Hall;

Locksley Hall, that half in ruin overlooks the sandy
    tracts,
And the hollow ocean-ridges roaring into cataracts.

Many a night from yonder ivied casement, ere I went
    to rest,
Did I look on great Orion sloping slowly to the West.

Many a night I saw the Pleiads, rising thro' the mellow
  shade,
Glitter like a swarm of fire-flies tangled in a silver
  braid.

Here about the beach I wander'd, nourishing a youth
  sublime
With the fairy tales of science, and the long result of
  Time;

When the centuries behind me like a fruitful land
  reposed;
When I clung to all the present for the promise that
  it closed:

When I dipt into the future far as human eye could
  see;
Saw the Vision of the world, and all the wonder that
  would be. ——

In the Spring a fuller crimson comes upon the robin's
  breast;
In the Spring the wanton lapwing gets himself another
  crest;

In the Spring a livelier iris changes on the burnish'd
 dove;
In the Spring a young man's fancy lightly turns to
 thoughts of love.

Then her cheek was pale and thinner than should be
 for one so young,
And her eyes on all my motions with a mute observance
 hung.

And I said, " My cousin Amy, speak, and speak the
 truth to me.
Trust me, cousin, all the current of my being sets to
 thee."

On her pallid cheek and forehead came a colour and
 a light,
As I have seen the rosy red flushing in the northern
 night.

And she turn'd—her bosom shaken with a sudden
 storm of sighs—
All the spirit deeply dawning in the dark of hazel
 eyes—

Saying, " I have hid my feelings, fearing they should
     do me wrong;"
Saying, " Dost thou love me, cousin ?" weeping, " I
     have loved thee long."

Love took up the glass of Time, and turn'd it in his
     glowing hands;
Every moment, lightly shaken, ran itself in golden
     sands.

Love took up the harp of Life, and smote on all the
     chords with might;
Smote the chord of Self, that, trembling, pass'd in
     music out of sight.

Many a morning on the moorland did we hear the
     copses ring,
And her whisper throng'd my pulses with the fullness
     of the Spring.

Many an evening by the waters did we watch the
     stately ships,
And our spirits rush'd together at the touching of the
     lips.

O my cousin, shallow-hearted !   O my Amy, mine no
    more !
O the dreary, dreary moorland !   O the barren, barren
    shore !

Falser than all fancy fathoms, falser than all songs
    have sung,
Puppet to a father's threat, and servile to a shrewish
    tongue !

Is it well to wish thee happy?—having known me—to
    decline
On a range of lower feelings and a narrower heart than
    mine !

Yet it shall be: thou shalt lower to his level day by
    day,
What is fine within thee growing coarse to sympathise
    with clay.

As the husband is, the wife is: thou art mated with a
    clown,
And the grossness of his nature will have weight to
    drag thee down.

He will hold thee, when his passion shall have spent
    its novel force,
Something better than his dog, a little dearer than his
    horse.

What is this? his eyes are heavy: think not they are
    glazed with wine.
Go to him: it is thy duty: kiss him: take his hand
    in thine.

It may be my lord is weary, that his brain is over-
    wrought:
Soothe him with thy finer fancies, touch him with thy
    lighter thought.

He will answer to the purpose, easy things to under-
    stand—
Better thou wert dead before me, tho' I slew thee with
    my hand !

Better thou and I were lying, hidden from the heart's
    disgrace,
Roll'd in one another's arms, and silent in a last
    embrace.

Cursed be the social wants that sin against the
    strength of youth !
Cursed be the social lies that warp us from the living
    truth !

Cursed be the sickly forms that err from honest
    Nature's rule !
Cursed be the gold that gilds the straiten'd forehead
    of the fool !

Well—'tis well that I should bluster !—Hadst thou
    less unworthy proved—
Would to God—for I had loved thee more than ever
    wife was loved.

Am I mad, that I should cherish that which bears but
    bitter fruit ?
I will pluck it from my bosom, tho' my heart be at
    the root.

Never, tho' my mortal summers to such length of
    years should come
As the many-winter'd crow that leads the clanging
    rookery home.

Where is comfort? in division of the records of the
  mind?
Can I part her from herself, and love her, as I knew
  her, kind?

I remember one that perish'd: sweetly did she speak
  and move:
Such a one do I remember, whom to look at was to
  love.

Can I think of her as dead, and love her for the love
  she bore?
No—she never loved me truly: love is love for evermore.

Comfort? comfort scorn'd of devils! this is truth the
  poet sings,
That a sorrow's crown of sorrow is remembering
  happier things.

Drug thy memories, lest thou learn it, lest thy heart
  be put to proof,
In the dead unhappy night, and when the rain is on
  the roof.

Like a dog, he hunts in dreams, and thou art staring
    at the wall,
Where the dying night-lamp flickers, and the shadows
    rise and fall.

Then a hand shall pass before thee, pointing to his
    drunken sleep,
To thy widow'd marriage-pillows, to the tears that
    thou wilt weep.

Thou shalt hear the " Never, never," whisper'd by the
    phantom years,
And a song from out the distance in the ringing of
    thine ears ;

And an eye shall vex thee, looking ancient kindness
    on thy pain.
Turn thee, turn thee on thy pillow : get thee to thy
    rest again.

Nay, but Nature brings thee solace ; for a tender
    voice will cry.
'Tis a purer life than thine ; a lip to drain thy trouble
    dry.

Baby lips will laugh me down : my latest rival brings
    thee rest.
Baby fingers, waxen touches, press me from the
    mother's breast.

O, the child too clothes the father with a dearness
    not his due.
Half is thine and half is his : it will be worthy of the
    two.

O, I see thee old and formal, fitted to thy petty
    part,
With a little hoard of maxims preaching down a
    daughter's heart.

" They were dangerous guides the feelings—she
    herself was not exempt—
Truly, she herself had suffer'd "—Perish in thy self-
    contempt !

Overlive it—lower yet—be happy ! wherefore should
    I care ?
I myself must mix with action, lest I wither by
    despair.

What is that which I should turn to, lighting upon
    days like these?
Every door is barr'd with gold, and opens but to
    golden keys.

Every gate is throng'd with suitors, all the markets
    overflow.
I have but an angry fancy: what is that which I
    should do?

I had been content to perish, falling on the foeman's
    ground,
When the ranks are roll'd in vapour, and the winds
    are laid with sound.

But the jingling of the guinea helps the hurt that
    Honour feels,
And the nations do but murmur, snarling at each
    other's heels.

Can I but relive in sadness?   I will turn that earlier
    page.
Hide me from my deep emotion, O thou wondrous
    Mother-Age!

Make me feel the wild pulsation that I felt before the
strife,
When I heard my days before me, and the tumult of
my life ;

Yearning for the large excitement that the coming
years would yield,
Eager-hearted as a boy when first he leaves his father's
field,

And at night along the dusky highway near and nearer
drawn,
Sees in heaven the light of London flaring like a dreary
dawn ;

And his spirit leaps within him to be gone before him
then,
Underneath the light he looks at, in among the throngs
of men ;

Men, my brothers, men the workers, ever reaping
something new :
That which they have done but earnest of the things
that they shall do :

For I dipt into the future, far as human eye could
    see,
Saw the Vision of the world, and all the wonder that
    would be;

Saw the heavens fill with commerce, argosies of magic
    sails,
Pilots of the purple twilight, dropping down with costly
    bales;

Heard the heavens fill with shouting, and there rain'd
    a ghastly dew
From the nations' airy navies grappling in the central
    blue;

Far along the world-wide whisper of the south-wind
    rushing warm,
With the standards of the peoples plunging thro' the
    thunder-storm;

Till the war-drum throbb'd no longer, and the battle-
    flags were furl'd
In the Parliament of man, the Federation of the
    world.

There the common sense of most shall hold a fretful
    realm in awe,
And the kindly earth shall slumber, lapt in universal
    law.

So I triumph'd ere my passion sweeping thro' me left
    me dry,
Left me with the palsied heart, and left me with the
    jaundiced eye;

Eye, to which all order festers, all things here are out
    of joint:
Science moves, but slowly slowly, creeping on from
    point to point:

Slowly comes a hungry people, as a lion, creeping
    nigher,
Glares at one that nods and winks behind a slowly-
    dying fire.

Yet I doubt not thro' the ages one increasing purpose
    runs,
And the thoughts of men are widen'd with the process
    of the suns.

What is that to him that reaps not harvest of his
    youthful joys,
Tho' the deep heart of existence beat for ever like a
    boy's?

Knowledge comes, but wisdom lingers, and I linger on
    the shore,
And the individual withers, and the world is more and
    more.

Knowledge comes, but wisdom lingers, and he bears a
    laden breast,
Full of sad experience, moving toward the stillness of
    his rest.

Hark, my merry comrades call me, sounding on the
    bugle-horn,
They to whom my foolish passion were a target for
    their scorn:

Shall it not be scorn to me to harp on such a moulder'd
    string?
I am shamed thro' all my nature to have loved so
    slight a thing.

Weakness to be wroth with weakness! woman's
    pleasure, woman's pain—
Nature made them blinder motions bounded in a
    shallower brain:

Woman is the lesser man, and all thy passions,
    match'd with mine,
Are as moonlight unto sunlight, and as water unto
    wine—

Here at least, where nature sickens, nothing. Ah, for
    some retreat
Deep in yonder shining Orient, where my life began
    to beat;

Where in wild Mahratta-battle fell my father evil-
    starr'd;—
I was left a trampled orphan, and a selfish uncle's
    ward.

Or to burst all links of habit—there to wander far
    away,
On from island unto island at the gateways of the
    day.

Larger constellations burning, mellow moons and
    happy skies,
Breadths of tropic shade and palms in cluster, knots
    of Paradise.

Never comes the trader, never floats an European
    flag,
Slides the bird o'er lustrous woodland, swings the
    trailer from the crag;

Droops the heavy-blossom'd bower, hangs the heavy-
    fruited tree—
Summer isles of Eden lying in dark-purple spheres of
    sea.

There methinks would be enjoyment more than in this
    march of mind,
In the steamship, in the railway, in the thoughts that
    shake mankind.

There the passions cramp'd no longer shall have scope
    and breathing-space;
I will take some savage woman, she shall rear my
    dusky race.

I

Iron-jointed, supple-sinew'd, they shall dive, and they
    shall run,
Catch the wild goat by the hair, and hurl their lances
    in the sun;

Whistle back the parrot's call, and leap the rainbows
    of the brooks,
Not with blinded eyesight poring over miserable
    books—

Fool, again the dream, the fancy! but I *know* my
    words are wild,
But I count the gray barbarian lower than the
    Christian child.

I, to herd with narrow foreheads, vacant of our glorious
    gains,
Like a beast with lower pleasures, like a beast with
    lower pains!

Mated with a squalid savage—what to me were sun
    or clime?
I the heir of all the ages, in the foremost files of
    time—

I that rather held it better men should perish one by
    one,
Than that earth should stand at gaze like Joshua's
    moon in Ajalon !

Not in vain the distance beacons.   Forward, forward
    let us range.
Let the great world spin for ever down the ringing
    grooves of change.

Thro' the shadow of the globe. we sweep into the
    younger day:
Better fifty years of Europe than a cycle of
    Cathay.

Mother-Age (for mine I knew not) help me as when
    life begun:
Rift the hills, and roll the waters, flash the lightnings,
    weigh the Sun—

O, I see the crescent promise of my spirit hath not
    set.
Ancient founts of inspiration well thro' all my fancy
    yet.

Howsoever these things be, a long farewell to Locksley
    Hall !
Now for me the woods may wither, now for me the
    roof-tree fall.

Comes a vapour from the margin, blackening over
    heath and holt,
Cramming all the blast before it, in its breast a
    thunderbolt.

Let it fall on Locksley Hall, with rain or hail, or fire
    or snow;
For the mighty wind arises, roaring seaward, and
    I go.

THE BROOK.

'HERE, by this brook, we parted; I to the East
And he for Italy—too late—too late:
One whom the strong sons of the world despise;
For lucky rhymes to him were scrip and share,
And mellow metres more than cent for cent;
Nor could he understand how money breeds,
Thought it a dead thing; yet himself could make
The thing that is not as the thing that is.
O had he lived! In our schoolbooks we say,
Of those that held their heads above the crowd,
They flourish'd then or then; but life in him
Could scarce be said to flourish, only touch'd
On such a time as goes before the leaf,
When all the wood stands in a mist of green,
And nothing perfect: yet the brook he loved,
For which, in branding summers of Bengal,
Or ev'n the sweet half-English Neilgherry air,

I panted, seems, as I re-listen to it,
Prattling the primrose fancies of the boy,
To me that loved him; for " O brook," he says,
" O babbling brook," says Edmund in his rhyme,
" Whence come you ?" and the brook, why not ? replies.

> I come from haunts of coot and hern,
>   I make a sudden sally
> And sparkle out among the fern,
>   To bicker down a valley.
>
> By thirty hills I hurry down,
>   Or slip between the ridges,
> By twenty thorps, a little town,
>   And half a hundred bridges.
>
> Till last by Philip's farm I flow
>   To join the brimming river,
> For men may come and men may go,
>   But I go on for ever.

' Poor lad, he died at Florence, quite worn out,
Travelling to Naples.   There is Darnley bridge,
It has more ivy; there the river; and there
Stands Philip's farm where brook and river meet.

> I chatter over stony ways,
>   In little sharps and trebles,
> I bubble into eddying bays,
>   I babble on the pebbles.

With many a curve my banks I fret
  By many a field and fallow,
And many a fairy foreland set
  With willow-weed and mallow.

I chatter, chatter, as I flow
  To join the brimming river,
For men may come and men may go,
  But I go on for ever.

'But Philip chatter'd more than brook or bird;
Old Philip; all about the fields you caught
His weary daylong chirping, like the dry
High-elbow'd grigs that leap in summer grass.

I wind about, and in and out,
  With here a blossom sailing,
And here and there a lusty trout,
  And here and there a grayling,

And here and there a foamy flake
  Upon me, as I travel
With many a silvery waterbreak
  Above the golden gravel,

And draw them all along, and flow
  To join the brimming river,
For men may come and men may go,
  But I go on for ever.

'O darling Katie Willows, his one child!
A maiden of our century, yet most meek;

A daughter of our meadows, yet not coarse;
Straight, but as lissome as a hazel wand;
Her eyes a bashful azure, and her hair
In gloss and hue the chestnut, when the shell
Divides threefold to show the fruit within.

  'Sweet Katie, once I did her a good turn,
Her and her far-off cousin and betrothed,
James Willows, of one name and heart with her.
For here I came, twenty years back—the week
Before I parted with poor Edmund; crost
By that old bridge which, half in ruins then,
Still makes a hoary eyebrow for the gleam
Beyond it, where the waters marry—crost,
Whistling a random bar of Bonny Doon,
And push'd at Philip's garden-gate. The gate,
Half-parted from a weak and scolding hinge,
Stuck; and he clamour'd from a casement, "run"
To Katie somewhere in the walks below,
"Run, Katie!" Katie never ran: she moved
To meet me, winding under woodbine bowers,
A little flutter'd, with her eyelids down,
Fresh apple-blossom, blushing for a boon.

  'What was it? less of sentiment than sense
Had Katie; not illiterate; nor of those

Who dabbling in the fount of fictive tears,
And nursed by mealy-mouth'd philanthropies,
Divorce the Feeling from her mate the Deed.

   'She told me.   She and James had quarrell'd.
      Why?
What cause of quarrel?   None, she said, no cause;
James had no cause: but when I prest the cause,
I learnt that James had flickering jealousies
Which anger'd her.   Who anger'd James? I said.
But Katie snatch'd her eyes at once from mine,
And sketching with her slender pointed foot
Some figure like a wizard's pentagram
On garden gravel, let my query pass
Unclaim'd, in flushing silence, till I ask'd
If James were coming.   "Coming every day,"
She answer'd, "ever longing to explain,
But evermore her father came across
With some long-winded tale, and broke him short;
And James departed vext with him and her."
How could I help her?   "Would I—was it wrong?"
(Claspt hands and that petitionary grace
Of sweet seventeen subdued me ere she spoke)
"O would I take her father for one hour,
For one half-hour, and let him talk to me!"
And even while she spoke, I saw where James

Made toward us, like a wader in the surf,
Beyond the brook, waist-deep in meadow-sweet.

'O Katie, what I suffer'd for your sake !
For in I went, and call'd old Philip out
To show the farm: full willingly he rose:
He led me thro' the short sweet-smelling lanes
Of his wheat-suburb, babbling as he went.
He praised his land, his horses, his machines;
He praised his ploughs, his cows, his hogs, his dogs;
He praised his hens, his geese, his guinea-hens;
His pigeons, who in session on their roofs
Approved him, bowing at their own deserts:
Then from the plaintive mother's teat he took
Her blind and shuddering puppies, naming each,
And naming those, his friends, for whom they were:
Then crost the common into Darnley chase
To show Sir Arthur's deer.   In copse and fern
Twinkled the innumerable ear and tail.
Then, seated on a serpent-rooted beech,
He pointed out a pasturing colt, and said:
"That was the four-year-old I sold the Squire."
And there he told a long long-winded tale
Of how the Squire had seen the colt at grass,
And how it was the thing his daughter wish'd,
And how he sent the bailiff to the farm

To learn the price, and what the price he ask'd,
And how the bailiff swore that he was mad,
But he stood firm; and so the matter hung;
He gave them line: and five days after that
He met the bailiff at the Golden Fleece,
Who then and there had offer'd something more,
But he stood firm; and so the matter hung;
He knew the man; the colt would fetch its price;
He gave them line: and how by chance at last
(It might be May or April, he forgot,
The last of April or the first of May)
He found the bailiff riding by the farm,
And, talking from the point, he drew him in,
And there he mellow'd all his heart with ale,
Until they closed a bargain, hand in hand.

'Then, while I breathed in sight of haven, he,
Poor fellow, could he help it? recommenced,
And ran thro' all the coltish chronicle,
Wild Will, Black Bess, Tantivy, Tallyho,
Reform, White Rose, Bellerophon, the Jilt,
Arbaces, and Phenomenon, and the rest,
Till, not to die a listener, I arose,
And with me Philip, talking still; and so
We turn'd our foreheads from the falling sun,
And following our own shadows thrice as long

As when they follow'd us from Philip's door,
Arrived, and found the sun of sweet content
Re-risen in Katie's eyes, and all things well.

> I steal by lawns and grassy plots,
>   I slide by hazel covers;
> I move the sweet forget-me-nots
>   That grow for happy lovers.
>
> I slip, I slide, I gloom, I glance,
>   Among my skimming swallows;
> I make the netted sunbeam dance
>   Against my sandy shallows.
>
> I murmur under moon and stars
>   In brambly wildernesses;
> I linger by my shingly bars;
>   I loiter round my cresses;
>
> And out again I curve and flow
>   To join the brimming river,
> For men may come and men may go,
>   But I go on for ever.

Yes, men may come and go; and these are gone,
All gone.   My dearest brother, Edmund, sleeps,
Not by the well-known stream and rustic spire,
But unfamiliar Arno, and the dome
Of Brunelleschi; sleeps in peace: and he,
Poor Philip, of all his lavish waste of words

Remains the lean P. W. on his tomb:
I scraped the lichen from it: Katie walks
By the long wash of Australasian seas
Far off, and holds her head to other stars,
And breathes in converse seasons.   All are gone.'

   So Lawrence Aylmer, seated on a style
In the long hedge, and rolling in his mind
Old waifs of rhyme, and bowing o'er the brook
A tonsured head in middle age forlorn,
Mused, and was mute.   On a sudden a low breath
Of tender air made tremble in the hedge
The fragile bindweed-bells and briony rings;
And he look'd up.   There stood a maiden near,
Waiting to pass.   In much amaze he stared
On eyes a bashful azure, and on hair
In gloss and hue the chestnut, when the shell
Divides threefold to show the fruit within:
Then, wondering, ask'd her 'Are you from the farm?'
'Yes' answer'd she.   'Pray stay a little: pardon me;
What do they call you?'   'Katie.'   'That were strange.
What surname?' 'Willows.' 'No!' 'That is my name.'
'Indeed!' and here he look'd so self-perplext,
That Katie laugh'd, and laughing blush'd, till he
Laugh'd also, but as one before he wakes,
Who feels a glimmering strangeness in his dream.

Then looking at her; 'Too happy, fresh and fair,
Too fresh and fair in our sad world's best bloom,
To be the ghost of one who bore your name
About these meadows, twenty years ago.'

'Have you not heard?' said Katie, 'we came back.
We bought the farm we tenanted before.
Am I so like her? so they said on board.
Sir, if you knew her in her English days,
My mother, as it seems you did, the days
That most she loves to talk of, come with me.
My brother James is in the harvest-field:
But she—you will be welcome—O, come in !'

EDWARD GRAY.

Sweet Emma Moreland of yonder town
  Met me walking on yonder way,
" And have you lost your heart ? " she said ;
  " And are you married yet, Edward Gray ? "

Sweet Emma Moreland spoke to me :
  Bitterly weeping I turn'd away :
" Sweet Emma Moreland, love no more
  Can touch the heart of Edward Gray.

" Ellen Adair she loved me well,
  Against her father's and mother's will :
To-day I sat for an hour and wept,
  By Ellen's grave, on the windy hill.

" Shy she was, and I thought her cold ;
  Thought her proud, and fled over the sea ;
Fill'd I was with folly and spite,
  When Ellen Adair was dying for me.

" Cruel, cruel the words I said !
   Cruelly came they back to-day :
' You're too slight and fickle,' I said,
   ' To trouble the heart of Edward Gray.'

" There I put my face in the grass—
   Whisper'd ' Listen to my despair :
I repent me of all I did :
   Speak a little, Ellen Adair !'

" Then I took a pencil, and wrote
   On the mossy stone, as I lay,
' Here lies the body of Ellen Adair ;
   And here the heart of Edward Gray !'

" Love may come, and love may go,
   And fly, like a bird, from tree to tree :
But I will love no more, no more,
   Till Ellen Adair come back to me.

" Bitterly wept I over the stone :
   Bitterly weeping I turn'd away :
There lies the body of Ellen Adair !
   And there the heart of Edward Gray !"

ŒNONE.

THERE lies a vale in Ida, lovelier
Than all the valleys of Ionian hills.
The swimming vapour slopes athwart the glen,
Puts forth an arm, and creeps from pine to pine,
And loiters, slowly drawn.   On either hand
The lawns and meadow-ledges midway down
Hang rich in bloom, and far below them roars
The long brook falling thro' the clov'n ravine
In cataract after cataract to the sea.
Behind the valley topmost Gargarus
Stands up and takes the morning : but in front
The gorges, opening wide apart, reveal
Troas and Ilion's column'd citadel,
The crown of Troas.

               Hither came at noon
Mournful Œnone, wandering forlorn
Of Paris, once her playmate on the hills.
Her cheek had lost the rose, and round her neck
Floated her hair or seem'd to float in rest.

K

She, leaning on a fragment twined with vine,
Sang to the stillness, till the mountain-shade
Sloped downward to her seat from the upper cliff.

"O mother Ida, many-fountain'd Ida,
Dear mother Ida, harken ere I die.
For now the noonday quiet holds the hill:
The grasshopper is silent in the grass:
The lizard, with his shadow on the stone,
Rests like a shadow, and the cicala sleeps.
The purple flowers droop: the golden bee
Is lily-cradled: I alone awake.
My eyes are full of tears, my heart of love,
My heart is breaking, and my eyes are dim,
And I am all aweary of my life.

"O mother Ida, many-fountain'd Ida,
Dear mother Ida, harken ere I die.
Hear me O Earth, hear me O Hills, O Caves
That house the cold crown'd snake! O mountain
          brooks,
I am the daughter of a River-God,
Hear me, for I will speak, and build up all
My sorrow with my song, as yonder walls
Rose slowly to a music slowly breathed,
A cloud that gather'd shape: for it may be

That, while I speak of it, a little while
My heart may wander from its deeper woe.

"O mother Ida, many-fountain'd Ida,
Dear mother Ida, harken ere I die.
I waited underneath the dawning hills,
Aloft the mountain lawn was dewy-dark,
And dewy-dark aloft the mountain pine :
Beautiful Paris, evil-hearted Paris,
Leading a jet-black goat white-horn'd, white-hooved,
Came up from reedy Simoïs all alone.

"O mother Ida, harken ere I die.
Far-off the torrent call'd me from the cleft :
Far up the solitary morning smote
The streaks of virgin snow.   With down-dropt eyes
I sat alone : white-breasted like a star
Fronting the dawn he moved ; a leopard skin
Droop'd from his shoulder, but his sunny hair
Cluster'd about his temples like a God's ;
And his cheek brighten'd as the foam-bow brightens
When the wind blows the foam, and all my heart
Went forth to embrace him coming ere he came.

"Dear mother Ida, harken ere I die.
He smiled, and opening out his milk-white palm

K 2

Disclosed a fruit of pure Hesperian gold,
That smelt ambrosially, and while I look'd
And listen'd, the full-flowing river of speech
Came down upon my heart.

      " ' My own Œnone,
Beautiful-brow'd Œnone, my own soul,
Behold this fruit, whose gleaming rind ingrav'n
" For the most fair," would seem to award it thine,
As lovelier than whatever Oread haunt
The knolls of Ida, loveliest in all grace
Of movement, and the charm of married brows.'

 " Dear mother Ida, harken ere I die.
He prest the blossom of his lips to mine,
And added ' This was cast upon the board,
When all the full-faced presence of the Gods
Ranged in the halls of Peleus ; whereupon
Rose feud, with question unto whom 'twere due:
But light-foot Iris brought it yester-eve,
Delivering, that to me, by common voice,
Elected umpire, Herè comes to-day,
Pallas and Aphrodite, claiming each
This meed of fairest. Thou, within the cave
Behind yon whispering tuft of oldest pine,
Mayst well behold them unbeheld, unheard
Hear all, and see thy Paris judge of Gods.'

"Dear mother Ida, harken ere I die.
It was the deep midnoon: one silvery cloud
Had lost his way between the piney sides
Of this long glen.   Then to the bower they came,
Naked they came to that smooth-swarded bower,
And at their feet the crocus brake like fire,
Violet, amaracus, and asphodel,
Lotos and lilies: and a wind arose,
And overhead the wandering ivy and vine,
This way and that, in many a wild festoon
Ran riot, garlanding the gnarled boughs
With bunch and berry and flower thro' and thro'.

"O mother Ida, harken ere I die.
On the tree-tops a crested peacock lit,
And o'er him flow'd a golden cloud, and lean'd
Upon him, slowly dropping fragrant dew.
Then first I heard the voice of her, to whom
Coming thro' Heaven, like a light that grows
Larger and clearer, with one mind the Gods
Rise up for reverence.   She to Paris made
Proffer of royal power, ample rule
Unquestion'd, overflowing revenue
Wherewith to embellish state, 'from many a vale
And river-sunder'd champaign clothed with corn,
Or labour'd mines undrainable of ore.

Honour,' she said, 'and homage, tax and toll,
From many an inland town and haven large,
Mast-throng'd beneath her shadowing citadel
In glassy bays among her tallest towers.'

  " O mother Ida, harken ere I die.
Still she spake on and still she spake of power,
' Which in all action is the end of all;
Power fitted to the season; wisdom-bred
And throned of wisdom—from all neighbour crowns
Alliance and allegiance, till thy hand
Fail from the sceptre-staff.   Such boon from me,
From me, Heaven's Queen, Paris, to thee king-born,
A shepherd all thy life but yet king-born,
Should come most welcome, seeing men, in power
Only, are likest gods, who have attain'd
Rest in a happy place and quiet seats
Above the thunder, with undying bliss
In knowledge of their own supremacy.'

  " Dear mother Ida, harken ere I die.
She ceased, and Paris held the costly fruit
Out at arm's-length, so much the thought of power
Flatter'd his spirit; but Pallas where she stood
Somewhat apart, her clear and bared limbs
O'erthwarted with the brazen-headed spear

Upon her pearly shoulder leaning cold,
The while, above, her full and earnest eye
Over her snow-cold breast and angry cheek
Kept watch, waiting decision, made reply.

"'Self-reverence, self-knowledge, self-control,
These three alone lead life to sovereign power.
Yet not for power, (power of herself
Would come uncall'd for) but to live by law,
Acting the law we live by without fear;
And, because right is right, to follow right
Were wisdom in the scorn of consequence.'

"Dear mother Ida, harken ere I die.
Again she said: 'I woo thee not with gifts.
Sequel of guerdon could not alter me
To fairer.   Judge thou me by what I am,
So shalt thou find me fairest.
                                Yet, indeed,
If gazing on divinity disrobed
Thy mortal eyes are frail to judge of fair,
Unbiass'd by self-profit, oh! rest thee sure
That I shall love thee well and cleave to thee,   ·
So that my vigour, wedded to thy blood,
Shall strike within thy pulses, like a God's,
To push thee forward thro' a life of shocks,

Dangers, and deeds, until endurance grow
Sinew'd with action, and the full-grown will,
Circled thro' all experiences, pure law,
Commeasure perfect freedom.'
                              "Here she ceased,
And Paris ponder'd, and I cried, 'O Paris,
Give it to Pallas!' but he heard me not,
Or hearing would not hear me, woe is me!

    "O mother Ida, many-fountain'd Ida,
Dear mother Ida, harken ere I die.
Idalian Aphrodite beautiful,
Fresh as the foam, new-bathed in Paphian wells,
With rosy slender fingers backward drew
From her warm brows and bosom her deep hair
Ambrosial, golden round her lucid throat
And shoulder: from the violets her light foot
Shone rosy-white, and o'er her rounded form
Between the shadows of the vine-bunches
Floated the glowing sunlights, as she moved.

    "Dear mother Ida, harken ere I die.
She with a subtle smile in her mild eyes,
The herald of her triumph, drawing nigh
Half-whisper'd in his ear, 'I promise thee
The fairest and most loving wife in Greece,'

She spoke and laugh'd: I shut my sight for fear:
But when I look'd, Paris had raised his arm,
And I beheld great Herè's angry eyes,
As she withdrew into the golden cloud,
And I was left alone within the bower;
And from that time to this I am alone,
And I shall be alone until I die.

"Yet, mother Ida, harken ere I die.
Fairest—why fairest wife? am I not fair?
My love hath told me so a thousand times.
Methinks I must be fair, for yesterday,
When I past by, a wild and wanton pard,
Eyed like the evening star, with playful tail
Crouch'd fawning in the weed. Most loving is she?
Ah me, my mountain shepherd, that my arms
Were wound about thee, and my hot lips prest
Close, close to thine in that quick-falling dew
Of fruitful kisses, thick as Autumn rains
Flash in the pools of whirling Simois.

"O mother, hear me yet before I die.
They came, they cut away my tallest pines,
My dark tall pines, that plumed the craggy ledge
High over the blue gorge, and all between
The snowy peak and snow-white cataract

Foster'd the callow eaglet—from beneath
Whose thick mysterious boughs in the dark morn
The panther's roar came muffled, while I sat
Low in the valley.   Never, never more
Shall lone Œnone see the morning mist
Sweep thro' them; never see them overlaid
With narrow moon-lit slips of silver cloud,
Between the loud stream and the trembling stars.

    "O mother, hear me yet before I die.
I wish that somewhere in the ruin'd folds,
Among the fragments tumbled from the glens,
Or the dry thickets, I could meet with her,
The Abominable, that uninvited came
Into the fair Peleïan banquet-hall,
And cast the golden fruit upon the board,
And bred this change; that I might speak my mind,
And tell her to her face how much I hate
Her presence, hated both of Gods and men.

    "O mother, hear me yet before I die.
Hath he not sworn his love a thousand times,
In this green valley, under this green hill,
Ev'n on this hand, and sitting on this stone?
Seal'd it with kisses? water'd it with tears?
O happy tears, and how unlike to these!

O happy Heaven, how canst thou see my face?
O happy earth, how canst thou bear my weight?
O death, death, death, thou ever-floating cloud,
There are enough unhappy on this earth,
Pass by the happy souls, that love to live:
I pray thee, pass before my light of life,
And shadow all my soul, that I may die.
Thou weighest heavy on the heart within,
Weigh heavy on my eyelids: let me die.

"O mother, hear me yet before I die.
I will not die alone, for fiery thoughts
Do shape themselves within me, more and more,
Whereof I catch the issue, as I hear
Dead sounds at night come from the inmost hills,
Like footsteps upon wool. I dimly see
My far-off doubtful purpose, as a mother
Conjectures of the features of her child
Ere it is born: her child!—a shudder comes
Across me: never child be born of me,
Unblest, to vex me with his father's eyes!

"O mother, hear me yet before I die.
Hear me, O earth. I will not die alone,
Lest their shrill happy laughter come to me
Walking the cold and starless road of Death

Uncomforted, leaving my ancient love
With the Greek woman.   I will rise and go
Down into Troy, and ere the stars come forth
Talk with the wild Cassandra, for she says
A fire dances before her, and a sound
Rings ever in her ears of armed men.
What this may be I know not, but I know
That, wheresoe'er I am by night and day,
All earth and air seem only burning fire."

TITHONUS.

THE woods decay, the woods decay and fall,
The vapours weep their burthen to the ground,
Man comes and tills the field and lies beneath,
And after many a summer dies the swan.
Me only cruel immortality
Consumes : I wither slowly in thine arms,
Here at the quiet limit of the world,
A white-hair'd shadow roaming like a dream
The ever silent spaces of the East,
Far-folded mists, and gleaming halls of morn.

Alas ! for this gray shadow, once a man—
So glorious in his beauty and thy choice,
Who madest him thy chosen, that he seem'd
To his great heart none other than a God !
I ask'd thee, ' Give me immortality.'
Then didst thou grant mine asking with a smile,
Like wealthy men who care not how they give.

But thy strong Hours indignant work'd their wills,
And beat me down and marr'd and wasted me,
And tho' they could not end me, left me maim'd
To dwell in presence of immortal youth,
Immortal age beside immortal youth,
And all I was, in ashes.   Can thy love,
Thy beauty, make amends, tho' even now,
Close over us, the silver star, thy guide,
Shines in those tremulous eyes that fill with tears
To hear me?   Let me go : take back thy gift :
Why should a man desire in any way
To vary from the kindly race of men,
Or pass beyond the goal of ordinance
Where all should pause, as is most meet for all?

A soft air fans the cloud apart; there comes
A glimpse of that dark world where I was born.
Once more the old mysterious glimmer steals
From thy pure brows, and from thy shoulders pure,
And bosom beating with a heart renew'd.
Thy cheek begins to redden thro' the gloom,
Thy sweet eyes brighten slowly close to mine,
Ere yet they blind the stars, and the wild team
Which love thee, yearning for thy yoke, arise,
And shake the darkness from their loosen'd manes,
And beat the twilight into flakes of fire.

Lo ! ever thus thou growest beautiful
In silence, then before thine answer given
Departest, and thy tears are on my cheek.

Why wilt thou ever scare me with thy tears,
And make me tremble lest a saying learnt,
In days far-off, on that dark earth, be true ?
' The Gods themselves cannot recall their gifts.'

Ay me ! ay me ! with what another heart
In days far-off, and with what other eyes
I used to watch—if I be he that watch'd—
The lucid outline forming round thee ; saw
The dim curls kindle into sunny rings ;
Changed with thy mystic change, and felt my blood
Glow with the glow that slowly crimson'd all
Thy presence and thy portals, while I lay,
Mouth, forehead, eyelids, growing dewy-warm
With kisses balmier than half-opening buds
Of April, and could hear the lips that kiss'd
Whispering I knew not what of wild and sweet,
Like that strange song I heard Apollo sing,
While Ilion like a mist rose into towers.

Yet hold me not for ever in thine East :
How can my nature longer mix with thine ?

Coldly thy rosy shadows bathe me, cold
Are all thy lights, and cold my wrinkled feet
Upon thy glimmering thresholds, when the steam
Floats up from those dim fields about the homes
Of happy men that have the power to die,
And grassy barrows of the happier dead.
Release me, and restore me to the ground;
Thou seëst all things, thou wilt see my grave:
Thou wilt renew thy beauty morn by morn;
I earth in earth forget these empty courts,
And thee returning on thy silver wheels.

ULYSSES.

It little profits that an idle king,
By this still hearth, among these barren crags,
Match'd with an aged wife, I mete and dole
Unequal laws unto a savage race,
That hoard, and sleep, and feed, and know not me.
I cannot rest from travel: I will drink
Life to the lees: all times I have enjoy'd
Greatly, have suffer'd greatly, both with those
That loved me, and alone; on shore, and when
Thro' scudding drifts the rainy Hyades
Vext the dim sea: I am become a name;
For always roaming with a hungry heart
Much have I seen and known; cities of men
And manners, climates, councils, governments,
Myself not least, but honour'd of them all;
And drunk delight of battle with my peers,
Far on the ringing plains of windy Troy.
I am a part of all that I have met;
Yet all experience is an arch wherethro'

L

Gleams that untravell'd world, whose margin fades
For ever and for ever when I move.
How dull it is to pause, to make an end,
To rust unburnish'd, not to shine in use !
As tho' to breathe were life.   Life piled on life
Were all too little, and of one to me
Little remains : but every hour is saved
From that eternal silence, something more,
A bringer of new things ; and vile it were
For some three suns to store and hoard myself,
And this gray spirit yearning in desire
To follow knowledge like a sinking star,
Beyond the utmost bound of human thought.
   This is my son, mine own Telemachus,
To whom I leave the sceptre and the isle—
Well-loved of me, discerning to fulfil
This labour, by slow prudence to make mild
A rugged people, and thro' soft degrees
Subdue them to the useful and the good.
Most blameless is he, centred in the sphere
Of common duties, decent not to fail
In offices of tenderness, and pay
Meet adoration to my household gods,
When I am gone.   He works his work, I mine.
   There lies the port : the vessel puffs her sail :
There gloom the dark broad seas.   My mariners,

Souls that have toil'd, and wrought, and thought with
      me—
That ever with a frolic welcome took
The thunder and the sunshine, and opposed
Free hearts, free foreheads—you and I are old;
Old age hath yet his honour and his toil;
Death closes all: but something ere the end,
Some work of noble note, may yet be done,
Not unbecoming men that strove with Gods.
The lights begin to twinkle from the rocks:
The long day wanes: the slow moon climbs: the deep
Moans round with many voices. Come, my friends,
'Tis not too late to seek a newer world.
Push off, and sitting well in order smite
The sounding furrows; for my purpose holds
To sail beyond the sunset, and the baths
Of all the western stars, until I die.
It may be that the gulfs will wash us down:
It may be we shall touch the Happy Isles,
And see the great Achilles, whom we knew.
Tho' much is taken, much abides; and tho'
We are not now that strength which in old days
Moved earth and heaven; that which we are, we are;
One equal temper of heroic hearts,
Made weak by time and fate, but strong in will
To strive, to seek, to find, and not to yield.

THE GOLDEN YEAR.

WELL, you shall have that song which Leonard wrote:
It was last summer on a tour in Wales:
Old James was with me: we that day had been
Up Snowdon; and I wish'd for Leonard there,
And found him in Llanberis: then we crost
Between the lakes, and clamber'd half way up
The counter side; and that same song of his
He told me; for I banter'd him, and swore
They said he lived shut up within himself,
A tongue-tied Poet in the feverous days,
That, setting the *how much* before the *how*,
Cry, like the daughters of the horseleech, " Give,
Cram us with all," but count not me the herd !
　　To which "They call me what they will," he said:
" But I was born too late : the fair new forms,
That float about the threshold of an age,
Like truths of Science waiting to be caught—
Catch me who can, and make the catcher crown'd—
Are taken by the forelock.　Let it be.
But if you care indeed to listen, hear
These measured words, my work of yestermorn.
　　"We sleep and wake and sleep, but all things move;
The Sun flies forward to his brother Sun;
The dark Earth follows wheel'd in her ellipse;
And human things returning on themselves

Move onward, leading up the golden year.
   "Ah, tho' the times, when some new thought can bud,
Are but as poets' seasons when they flower,
Yet seas, that daily gain upon the shore,
Have ebb and flow conditioning their march,
And slow and sure comes up the golden year.
   "When wealth no more shall rest in mounded heaps,
But smit with freer light shall slowly melt
In many streams to fatten lower lands,
And light shall spread, and man be liker man
Thro' all the season of the golden year.
   " Shall eagles not be eagles? wrens be wrens?
If all the world were falcons, what of that?
The wonder of the eagle were the less,
But he not less the eagle.   Happy days
Roll onward, leading up the golden year.
   " Fly, happy happy sails and bear the Press;
Fly happy with the mission of the Cross;
Knit land to land, and blowing havenward
With silks, and fruits, and spices, clear of toll,
Enrich the markets of the golden year.
   " But we grow old.   Ah ! when shall all men's good
Be each man's rule, and universal Peace
Lie like a shaft of light across the land,
And like a lane of beams athwart the sea,
Thro' all the circle of the golden year?"

Thus far he flow'd, and ended; whereupon
"Ah, folly!" in mimic cadence answer'd James—
"Ah, folly! for it lies so far away,
Not in our time, nor in our children's time,
'Tis like the second world to us that live;
'Twere all as one to fix our hopes on Heaven
As on this vision of the golden year."
    With that he struck his staff against the rocks
And broke it,—James,—you know him,—old, but full
Of force and choler, and firm upon his feet,
And like an oaken stock in winter woods,
O'erflourish'd with the hoary clematis:
Then added, all in heat:
                                    " What stuff is this!
Old writers push'd the happy season back,—
The more fools they,—we forward: dreamers both:
You most, that in an age, when every hour
Must sweat her sixty minutes to the death,
Live on, God love us, as if the seedsman, rapt
Upon the teeming harvest, should not plunge
His hand into the bag: but well I know
That unto him who works, and feels he works,
This same grand year is ever at the doors."
    He spoke; and, high above, I heard them blast
The steep slate-quarry, and the great echo flap
And buffet round the hills from bluff to bluff.

THE VISION OF SIN.

1.

I HAD a vision when the night was late:
A youth came riding toward a palace-gate.
He rode a horse with wings, that would have flown,
But that his heavy rider kept him down.
And from the palace came a child of sin,
And took him by the curls, and led him in,
Where sat a company with heated eyes,
Expecting when a fountain should arise:
A sleepy light upon their brows and lips—
As when the sun, a crescent of eclipse,
Dreams over lake and lawn, and isles and capes—
Suffused them, sitting, lying, languid shapes,
By heaps of gourds, and skins of wine, and piles of grapes.

2.

Then methought I heard a mellow sound,
Gathering up from all the lower ground;
Narrowing in to where they sat assembled
Low voluptuous music winding trembled,

Wov'n in circles: they that heard it sigh'd,
Panted hand in hand with faces pale,
Swung themselves, and in low tones replied;
Till the fountain spouted, showering wide
Sleet of diamond-drift and pearly hail;
Then the music touch'd the gates and died;
Rose again from where it seem'd to fail,
Storm'd in orbs of song, a growing gale;
Till thronging in and in, to where they waited,
As 'twere a hundred-throated nightingale,
The strong tempestuous treble throbb'd and palpitated;
Ran into its giddiest whirl of sound,
Caught the sparkles, and in circles,
Purple gauzes, golden hazes, liquid mazes,
Flung the torrent rainbow round:
Then they started from their places,
Moved with violence, changed in hue,
Caught each other with wild grimaces,
Half-invisible to the view,
Wheeling with precipitate paces
To the melody, till they flew,
Hair, and eyes, and limbs, and faces,
Twisted hard in fierce embraces,
Like to Furies, like to Graces,
Dash'd together in blinding dew:
Till, kill'd with some luxurious agony,

The nerve-dissolving melody
Flutter'd headlong from the sky.

3.

And then I look'd up toward a mountain-tract,
That girt the region with high cliff and lawn:
I saw that every morning, far withdrawn
Beyond the darkness and the cataract,
God made himself an awful rose of dawn,
Unheeded: and detaching, fold by fold,
From those still heights, and, slowly drawing near,
A vapour heavy, hueless, formless, cold,
Came floating on for many a month and year,
Unheeded: and I thought I would have spoken,
And warn'd that madman ere it grew too late:
But, as in dreams, I could not.   Mine was broken,
When that cold vapour touch'd the palace gate,
And link'd again.   I saw within my head
A gray and gap-tooth'd man as lean as death,
Who slowly rode across a wither'd heath,
And lighted at a ruin'd inn, and said:

4

" Wrinkled ostler, grim and thin !
    Here is custom come your way;
Take my brute, and lead him in,
    Stuff his ribs with mouldy hay.

" Bitter barmaid, waning fast !
    See that sheets are on my bed;
What ! the flower of life is past:
    It is long before you wed.

" Slip-shod waiter, lank and sour,
    At the Dragon on the heath !
Let us have a quiet hour,
    Let us hob-and-nob with Death.

" I am old, but let me drink ;
    Bring me spices, bring me wine ;
I remember, when I think,
    That my youth was half divine.

" Wine is good for shrivell'd lips,
    When a blanket wraps the day,
When the rotten woodland drips,
    And the leaf is stamp'd in clay.

" Sit thee down, and have no shame,
    Cheek by jowl, and knee by knee :
What care I for any name ?
    What for order or degree ?

" Let me screw thee up a peg :
    Let me loose thy tongue with wine :
Callest thou that thing a leg ?
    Which is thinnest ? thine or mine ?

" Thou shalt not be saved by works :
   Thou hast been a sinner too :
Ruin'd trunks on wither'd forks,
   Empty scarecrows, I and you !

" Fill the cup, and fill the can :
   Have a rouse before the morn :
Every moment dies a man,
   Every moment one is born.

" We are men of ruin'd blood ;
   Therefore comes it we are wise.
Fish are we that love the mud,
   Rising to no fancy-flies.

" Name and fame ! to fly sublime
   Thro' the courts, the camps, the schools,
Is to be the ball of Time,
   Bandied by the hands of fools.

" Friendship !—to be two in one—
   Let the canting liar pack !
Well I know, when I am gone,
   How she mouths behind my back.

" Virtue !—to be good and just—
   Every heart, when sifted well,
Is a clot of warmer dust,
   Mix'd with cunning sparks of hell.

"O! we two as well can look
   Whited thought and cleanly life
As the priest, above his book
   Leering at his neighbour's wife.

"Fill the cup, and fill the can:
   Have a rouse before the morn:
Every moment dies a man,
   Every moment one is born.

"Drink, and let the parties rave:
   They are fill'd with idle spleen;
Rising, falling, like a wave,
   For they know not what they mean.

"He that roars for liberty
   Faster binds a tyrant's power;
And the tyrant's cruel glee
   Forces on the freer hour.

"Fill the can, and fill the cup:
   All the windy ways of men
Are but dust that rises up,
   And is lightly laid again.

"Greet her with applausive breath,
   Freedom, gaily doth she tread;
In her right a civic wreath,
   In her left a human head.

" No, I love not what is new ;
  She is of an ancient house :
And I think we know the hue
  Of that cap upon her brows.

" Let her go ! her thirst she slakes
  Where the bloody conduit runs :
Then her sweetest meal she makes
  On the first-born of her sons.

" Drink to lofty hopes that cool—
  Visions of a perfect State :
Drink we, last, the public fool,
  Frantic love and frantic hate.

" Chant me now some wicked stave,
  Till thy drooping courage rise,
And the glow-worm of the grave
  Glimmer in thy rheumy eyes.

" Fear not thou to loose thy tongue ;
  Set thy hoary fancies free ;
What is loathsome to the young
  Savours well to thee and me.

" Change, reverting to the years,
  When thy nerves could understand
What there is in loving tears,
  And the warmth of hand in hand.

" Tell me tales of thy first love—
    April hopes, the fools of chance ;
Till the graves begin to move,
    And the dead begin to dance.

" Fill the can, and fill the cup :
    All the windy ways of men
Are but dust that rises up,
    And is lightly laid again.

" Trooping from their mouldy dens
    The chap-fallen circle spreads :
Welcome, fellow-citizens,
    Hollow hearts and empty heads !

" You are bones, and what of that ?
    Every face, however full,
Padded round with flesh and fat,
    Is but modell'd on a skull.

" Death is king, and Vivat Rex !
    Tread a measure on the stones,
Madam—if I know your sex,
    From the fashion of your bones.

" No, I cannot praise the fire
    In your eye—nor yet your lip :
All the more do I admire
    Joints of cunning workmanship.

" Lo ! God's likeness—the ground-plan—
    Neither modell'd, glazed, or framed:
Buss me, thou rough sketch of man,
    Far too naked to be shamed !

" Drink to Fortune, drink to Chance,
    While we keep a little breath !
Drink to heavy Ignorance !
    Hob-and-nob with brother Death !

" Thou art mazed, the night is long,
    And the longer night is near:
What ! I am not all as wrong
    As a bitter jest is dear.

" Youthful hopes, by scores, to all,
    When the locks are crisp and curl'd; ·
Unto me my maudlin gall
    And my mockeries of the world.

" Fill the cup, and fill the can !
    Mingle madness, mingle scorn !
Dregs of life, and lees of man:
    Yet we will not die forlorn."

5.

The voice grew faint: there came a further change:
Once more uprose the mystic mountain-range:

Below were men and horses pierced with worms,
And slowly quickening into lower forms ;
By shards and scurf of salt, and scum of dross,
Old plash of rains, and refuse patch'd with moss.
Then some one spake: " Behold ! it was a crime
Of sense avenged by sense that wore with time."
Another answer'd " But a crime of sense ?"
"Give him new nerves with old experience."
Another said: " The crime of sense became
The crime of malice, and is equal blame."
And one: " He had not wholly quench'd his power;
A little grain of conscience made him sour."
At last I heard a voice upon the slope
Cry to the summit, " Is there any hope ?"
To which an answer peal'd from that high land,
But in a tongue no man could understand;
And on the glimmering limit far withdrawn
God made Himself an awful rose of dawn.

MORTE D'ARTHUR.

So all day long the noise of battle roll'd
Among the mountains by the winter sea;
Until King Arthur's table, man by man,
Had fall'n in Lyonness about their Lord,
King Arthur: then, because his wound was deep,
The bold Sir Bedivere uplifted him,
Sir Bedivere, the last of all his knights,
And bore him to a chapel nigh the field,
A broken chancel with a broken cross,
That stood on a dark strait of barren land.
On one side lay the Ocean, and on one
Lay a great water, and the moon was full.
  Then spake King Arthur to Sir Bedivere:
" The sequel of to-day unsolders all
The goodliest fellowship of famous knights
Whereof this world holds record.   Such a sleep
They sleep—the men I loved.   I think that we
Shall never more, at any future time,
Delight our souls with talk of knightly deeds,

Walking about the gardens and the halls
Of Camelot, as in the days that were.
I perish by this people which I made,—
Tho' Merlin sware that I should come again
To rule once more—but let what will be, be,
I am so deeply smitten thro' the helm
That without help I cannot last till morn.
Thou therefore take my brand Excalibur,
Which was my pride: for thou rememberest how
In those old days, one summer noon, an arm
Rose up from out the bosom of the lake,
Clothed in white samite, mystic, wonderful,
Holding the sword—and how I row'd across
And took it, and have worn it, like a king:
And, wheresoever I am sung or told
In aftertime, this also shall be known:
But now delay not: take Excalibur,
And fling him far into the middle mere:
Watch what thou seëst, and lightly bring me word."
    To him replied the bold Sir Bedivere:
" It is not meet, Sir King, to leave thee thus,
Aidless, alone, and smitten thro' the helm.
A little thing may harm a wounded man.
Yet I thy hest will all perform at full,
Watch what I see, and lightly bring thee word."
    So saying, from the ruin'd shrine he stept

And in the moon athwart the place of tombs,
Where lay the mighty bones of ancient men,
Old knights, and over them the sea-wind sang
Shrill, chill, with flakes of foam.   He, stepping down
By zig-zag paths, and juts of pointed rock,
Came on the shining levels of the lake.
    There drew he forth the brand Excalibur,
And o'er him, drawing it, the winter moon,
Brightening the skirts of a long cloud, ran forth
And sparkled keen with frost against the hilt:
For all the haft twinkled with diamond sparks,
Myriads of topaz-lights, and jacinth-work
Of subtlest jewellery.   He gazed so long
That both his eyes were dazzled, as he stood,
This way and that dividing the swift mind,
In act to throw: but at the last it seem'd
Better to leave Excalibur conceal'd
There in the many-knotted waterflags,
That whistled stiff and dry about the marge.
So strode he back slow to the wounded King.
    Then spake King Arthur to Sir Bedivere:
"Hast thou perform'd my mission which I gave?
What is it thou hast seen? or what hast heard?"
    And answer made the bold Sir Bedivere:
"I heard the ripple washing in the reeds,
And the wild water lapping on the crag."

To whom replied King Arthur, faint and pale:
"Thou hast betray'd thy nature and thy name,
Not rendering true answer, as beseem'd
Thy fealty, nor like a noble knight:
For surer sign had follow'd, either hand,
Or voice, or else a motion of the mere.
This is a shameful thing for men to lie.
Yet now, I charge thee, quickly go again
As thou art lief and dear, and do the thing
I bad thee, watch, and lightly bring me word."
  Then went Sir Bedivere the second time
Across the ridge, and paced beside the mere,
Counting the dewy pebbles, fix'd in thought;
But when he saw the wonder of the hilt,
How curiously and strangely chased, he smote
His palms together, and he cried aloud.
  "And if indeed I cast the brand away,
Surely a precious thing, one worthy note,
Should thus be lost for ever from the earth,
Which might have pleased the eyes of many men.
What good should follow this, if this were done?
What harm, undone? deep harm to disobey,
Seeing obedience is the bond of rule.
Were it well to obey then, if a king demand
An act unprofitable, against himself?
The King is sick, and knows not what he does.

What record, or what relic of my lord
Should be to aftertime, but empty breath
And rumours of a doubt? but were this kept,
Stored in some treasure-house of mighty kings,
Some one might show it at a joust of arms,
Saying, 'King Arthur's sword, Excalibur,
Wrought by the lonely maiden of the Lake.
Nine years she wrought it, sitting in the deeps
Upon the hidden bases of the hills.'
So might some old man speak in the aftertime
To all the people, winning reverence.
But now much honour and much fame were lost."
   So spake he, clouded with his own conceit,
And hid Excalibur the second time,
And so strode back slow to the wounded King.
   Then spoke King Arthur, breathing heavily:
"What is it thou hast seen? or what hast heard?"
   And answer made the bold Sir Bedivere:
"I heard the water lapping on the crag,
And the long ripple washing in the reeds."
   To whom replied King Arthur, much in wrath:
"Ah, miserable and unkind, untrue,
Unknightly, traitor-hearted! Woe is me!
Authority forgets a dying king,
Laid widow'd of the power in his eye
That bow'd the will. I see thee what thou art,

For thou, the latest-left of all my knights,
In whom should meet the offices of all,
Thou wouldst betray me for the precious hilt;
Either from lust of gold, or like a girl
Valuing the giddy pleasure of the eyes.
Yet, for a man may fail in duty twice,
And the third time may prosper, get thee hence:
But, if thou spare to fling Excalibur,
I will arise and slay thee with my hands."
    Then quickly rose Sir Bedivere, and ran,
And, leaping down the ridges lightly, plunged
Among the bulrush-beds, and clutch'd the sword,
And strongly wheel'd and threw it.   The great brand
Made lightnings in the splendour of the moon,
And flashing round and round, and whirl'd in an arch,
Shot like a streamer of the northern morn,
Seen where the moving isles of winter shock
By night, with noises of the northern sea.
So flash'd and fell the brand Excalibur:
But ere he dipt the surface, rose an arm
Clothed in white samite, mystic, wonderful,
And caught him by the hilt, and brandish'd him
Three times, and drew him under in the mere.
And lightly went the other to the King.
    Then spoke King Arthur, drawing thicker breath:
"Now see I by thine eyes that this is done.

Speak out: what is it thou hast heard, or seen?"
And answer made the bold Sir Bedivere:
"Sir King, I closed mine eyelids, lest the gems
Should blind my purpose, for I never saw,
Nor shall see, here or elsewhere, till I die,
Not tho' I live three lives of mortal men,
So great a miracle as yonder hilt.
Then with both hands I flung him, wheeling him;
But when I look'd again, behold an arm,
Clothed in white samite, mystic, wonderful,
That caught him by the hilt, and brandish'd him
Three times, and drew him under in the mere."
And answer made King Arthur, breathing hard:
"My end draws nigh; 'tis time that I were gone.
Make broad thy shoulders to receive my weight,
And bear me to the margin; yet I fear
My wound hath taken cold, and I shall die."
So saying, from the pavement he half rose,
Slowly, with pain, reclining on his arm,
And looking wistfully with wide blue eyes
As in a picture.   Him Sir Bedivere
Remorsefully regarded thro' his tears,
And would have spoken, but he found not words,
Then took with care, and kneeling on one knee,
O'er both his shoulders drew the languid hands,
And rising bore him thro' the place of tombs.

But, as he walk'd, King Arthur panted hard,
Like one that feels a nightmare on his bed
When all the house is mute.   So sigh'd the King,
Muttering and murmuring at his ear "Quick, quick!
I fear it is too late, and I shall die."
But the other swiftly strode from ridge to ridge,
Clothed with his breath, and looking, as he walk'd,
Larger than human on the frozen hills.
He heard the deep behind him, and a cry
Before.   His own thought drove him like a goad.
Dry clash'd his harness in the icy caves
And barren chasms, and all to left and right
The bare black cliff clang'd round him, as he based
His feet on juts of slippery crag that rang
Sharp-smitten with the dint of armed heels—
And on a sudden, lo ! the level lake,
And the long glories of the winter moon.
    Then saw they how there hove a dusky barge,
Dark as a funeral scarf from stem to stern,
Beneath them; and descending they were ware
That all the decks were dense with stately forms
Black-stoled, black-hooded, like a dream—by these
Three Queens with crowns of gold—and from them rose
A cry that shiver'd to the tingling stars,
And, as it were one voice, an agony
Of lamentation, like a wind, that shrills

All night in a waste land, where no one comes,
Or hath come, since the making of the world.
   Then murmur'd Arthur, "Place me in the barge,"
And to the barge they came. There those three Queens
Put forth their hands, and took the King, and wept.
But she, that rose the tallest of them all
And fairest, laid his head upon her lap,
And loosed the shatter'd casque, and chafed his hands,
And call'd him by his name, complaining loud,
And dropping bitter tears against his brow
Striped with dark blood: for all his face was white
And colourless, and like the wither'd moon
Smote by the fresh beam of the springing east;
And all his greaves and cuisses dash'd with drops
Of onset; and the light and lustrous curls—
That made his forehead like a rising sun
High from the dais-throne—were parch'd with dust;
Or, clotted into points and hanging loose,
Mix'd with the knightly growth that fringed his lips.
So like a shatter'd column lay the King;
Not like that Arthur who, with lance in rest,
From spur to plume a star of tournament, .
Shot thro' the lists at Camelot, and charged
Before the eyes of ladies and of kings.
   Then loudly cried the bold Sir Bedivere,
"Ah ! my Lord Arthur, whither shall I go?

Where shall I hide my forehead and my eyes?
For now I see the true old times are dead,
When every morning brought a noble chance,
And every chance brought out a noble knight.
Such times have been not since the light that led
The holy Elders with the gift of myrrh.
But now the whole ROUND TABLE is dissolved
Which was an image of the mighty world;
And I, the last, go forth companionless,
And the days darken round me, and the years,
Among new men, strange faces, other minds."
    And slowly answered Arthur from the barge:
"The old order changeth, yielding place to new,
And God fulfils himself in many ways,
Lest one good custom should corrupt the world.
Comfort thyself: what comfort is in me?
I have lived my life, and that which I have done
May He within himself make pure! but thou,
If thou shouldst never see my face again,
Pray for my soul.   More things are wrought by prayer
Than this world dreams of.   Wherefore, let thy voice
Rise like a fountain for me night and day.
For what are men better than sheep or goats
That nourish a blind life within the brain,
If, knowing God, they lift not hands of prayer
Both for themselves and those who call them friend?

For so the whole round earth is every way
Bound by gold chains about the feet of God.
But now farewell. I am going a long way
With these thou seëst—if indeed I go—
(For all my mind is clouded with a doubt)
To the island-valley of Avilion;
Where falls not hail, or rain, or any snow,
Nor ever wind blows loudly; but it lies
Deep-meadow'd, happy, fair with orchard-lawns
And bowery hollows crown'd with summer sea,
Where I will heal me of my grievous wound."
  So said he, and the barge with oar and sail
Moved from the brink, like some full-breasted swan
That, fluting a wild carol ere her death,
Ruffles her pure cold plume, and takes the flood
With swarthy webs. Long stood Sir Bedivere
Revolving many memories, till the hull
Look'd one black dot against the verge of dawn,
And on the mere the wailing died away.

ODE ON THE DEATH OF THE DUKE OF WELLINGTON.

1852.

1.

BURY the Great Duke
  With an empire's lamentation,
Let us bury the Great Duke
  To the noise of the mourning of a mighty nation,
Mourning when their leaders fall,
Warriors carry the warrior's pall,
And sorrow darkens hamlet and hall.

2.

Where shall we lay the man whom we deplore?
Here, in streaming London's central roar.
Let the sound of those he wrought for,
And the feet of those he fought for,
Echo round his bones for evermore.

3.

Lead out the pageant: sad and slow,
As fits an universal woe,

Let the long long procession go,
And let the sorrowing crowd about it grow,
And let the mournful martial music blow;
The last great Englishman is low.

4.

Mourn, for to us he seems the last,
Remembering all his greatness in the Past.
No more in soldier fashion will he greet
With lifted hand the gazer in the street.
O friends, our chief state-oracle is mute:
Mourn for the man of long-enduring blood,
The statesman-warrior, moderate, resolute,
Whole in himself, a common good.
Mourn for the man of amplest influence,
Yet clearest of ambitious crime,
Our greatest yet with least pretence,
Great in council and great in war,
Foremost captain of his time,
Rich in saving common-sense,
And, as the greatest only are,
In his simplicity sublime.
O good gray head which all men knew,
O voice from which their omens all men drew,
O iron nerve to true occasion true,
O fall'n at length that tower of strength

Which stood four-square to all the winds that blew!
Such was he whom we deplore.
The long self-sacrifice of life is o'er.
The great World-victor's victor will be seen no more.

5.

All is over and done:
Render thanks to the Giver,
England, for thy son.
Let the bell be toll'd.
Render thanks to the Giver,
And render him to the mould.
Under the cross of gold
That shines over city and river,
There he shall rest for ever
Among the wise and the bold.
Let the bell be toll'd:
And a reverent people behold
The towering car, the sable steeds:
Bright let it be with its blazon'd deeds,
Dark in its funeral fold.
Let the bell be toll'd:
And a deeper knell in the heart be knoll'd;
And the sound of the sorrowing anthem roll'd
Thro' the dome of the golden cross;
And the volleying cannon thunder his loss;

He knew their voices of old.
For many a time in many a clime
His captain's-ear has heard them boom
Bellowing victory, bellowing doom :
When he with those deep voices wrought,
Guarding realms and kings from shame ;
With those deep voices our dead captain taught
The tyrant, and asserts his claim
In that dread sound to the great name,
Which he has worn so pure of blame,
In praise and in dispraise the same,
A man of well-attemper'd frame.
O civic muse, to such a name,
To such a name for ages long,
To such a name,
Preserve a broad approach of fame,
And ever-echoing avenues of song.

6.

Who is he that cometh, like an honour'd guest,
With banner and with music, with soldier and with
          priest,
With a nation weeping, and breaking on my rest ?
Mighty Seaman, this is he
Was great by land as thou by sea.
Thy country loves thee well, thou famous man,

The greatest sailor since our world began.
Now, to the roll of muffled drums,
To thee the greatest soldier comes;
For this is he,
Was great by land as thou by sea;
His foes were thine; he kept us free;
O give him welcome, this is he
Worthy of our gorgeous rites,
And worthy to be laid by thee;
For this is England's greatest son,
He that gain'd a hundred fights,
Nor ever lost an English gun;
This is he that far away
Against the myriads of Assaye
Clash'd with his fiery few and won;
And underneath another sun,
Warring on a later day,
Round affrighted Lisbon drew
The treble works, the vast designs
Of his labour'd rampart-lines,
Where he greatly stood at bay,
Whence he issued forth anew,
And ever great and greater grew,
Beating from the wasted vines
Back to France her banded swarms,
Back to France with countless blows,

Till o'er the hills her eagles flew
Beyond the Pyrenean pines,
Follow'd up in valley and glen
With blare of bugle, clamour of men,
Roll of cannon and clash of arms,
And England pouring on her foes.
Such a war had such a close.
Again their ravening eagle rose
In anger, wheel'd on Europe-shadowing wings,
And barking for the thrones of kings ;
Till one that sought but Duty's iron crown
On that loud sabbath shook the spoiler down ;
A day of onsets of despair !
Dash'd on every rocky square
Their surging charges foam'd themselves away ;
Last, the Prussian trumpet blew ;
Thro' the long-tormented air
Heaven flash'd a sudden jubilant ray,
And down we swept and charged and overthrew.
So great a soldier taught us there,
What long-enduring hearts could do
In that world's-earthquake, Waterloo !
Mighty Seaman, tender and true,
And pure as he from taint of craven guile,
O saviour of the silver-coasted isle,
O shaker of the Baltic and the Nile,

N

If aught of things that here befall
Touch a spirit among things divine,
If love of country move thee there at all,
Be glad, because his bones are laid by thine!
And thro' the centuries let a people's voice
In full acclaim,
A people's voice,
The proof and echo of all human fame,
A people's voice, when they rejoice
At civic revel and pomp and game,
Attest their great commander's claim
With honour, honour, honour, honour to him,
Eternal honour to his name.

7.

A people's voice ! we are a people yet.
Tho' all men else their nobler dreams forget,
Confused by brainless mobs and lawless Powers;
Thank Him who isled us here, and roughly set
His Briton in blown seas and storming showers,
We have a voice, with which to pay the debt
Of boundless love and reverence and regret
To those great men who fought, and kept it ours.
And keep it ours, O God, from brute control;
O Statesmen, guard us, guard the eye, the soul
Of Europe, keep our noble England whole,

And save the one true seed of freedom sown
Betwixt a people and their ancient throne,
That sober freedom out of which there springs
Our loyal passion for our temperate kings;
For, saving that, ye help to save mankind
Till public wrong be crumbled into dust,
And drill the raw world for the march of mind,   .
Till crowds at length be sane and crowns be just.
But wink no more in slothful overtrust.
Remember him who led your hosts;
He bad you guard the sacred coasts.
Your cannons moulder on the seaward wall;
His voice is silent in your council-hall
For ever; and whatever tempests lour
For ever silent; even if they broke
In thunder, silent; yet remember all
He spoke among you, and the Man who spoke;
Who never sold the truth to serve the hour,
Nor palter'd with Eternal God for power;
Who let the turbid streams of rumour flow
Thro' either babbling world of high and low;
Whose life was work, whose language rife
With rugged maxims hewn from life;
Who never spoke against a foe;
Whose eighty winters freeze with one rebuke
All great self-seekers trampling on the right:

Truth-teller was our England's Alfred named;
Truth-lover was our English Duke;
Whatever record leap to light
He never shall be shamed.

8.

.Lo, the leader in these glorious wars
Now to glorious burial slowly borne,
Follow'd by the brave of other lands,
He, on whom from both her open hands
Lavish Honour shower'd all her stars,
And affluent Fortune emptied all her horn.
Yea, let all good things await
Him who cares not to be great,
But as he saves or serves the state.
Not once or twice in our rough island-story,
The path of duty was the way to glory:
He that walks it, only thirsting
For the right, and learns to deaden
Love of self, before his journey closes,
He shall find the stubborn thistle bursting
Into glossy purples, which outredden
All voluptuous garden-roses.
Not once or twice in our fair island-story,
The path of duty was the way to glory:
He, that ever following her commands,

On with toil of heart and knees and hands,
Thro' the long gorge to the far light has won
His path upward, and prevail'd,
Shall find the toppling crags of Duty scaled
Are close upon the shining table-lands
To which our God Himself is moon and sun.
Such was he: his work is done,
But while the races of mankind endure,
Let his great example stand
Colossal, seen of every land,
And keep the soldier firm, the statesman pure;
Till in all lands and thro' all human story
The path of duty be the way to glory:
And let the land whose hearths he saved from shame
For many and many an age proclaim
At civic revel and pomp and game,
And when the long-illumined cities flame,
Their ever-loyal iron leader's fame,
With honour, honour, honour, honour to him,
Eternal honour to his name.

9.

Peace, his triumph will be sung
By some yet unmoulded tongue
Far on in summers that we shall not see:
Peace, it is a day of pain

For one about whose patriarchal knee
Late the little children clung:
O peace, it is a day of pain
For one, upon whose hand and heart and brain
Once the weight and fate of Europe hung.
Ours the pain, be his the gain !
More than is of man's degree
Must be with us, watching here
At this, our great solemnity.
Whom we see not we revere;
We revere, and we refrain
From talk of battles loud and vain,
And brawling memories all too free
For such a wise humility
As befits a solemn fane:
We revere, and while we hear
The tides of Music's golden sea
Setting toward eternity,
Uplifted high in heart and hope are we,
Until we doubt not that for one so true
There must be other nobler work to do
Than when he fought at Waterloo,
And Victor he must ever be.
For tho' the Giant Ages heave the hill
And break the shore, and evermore
Make and break, and work their will;

Tho' world on world in myriad myriads roll
Round us, each with different powers,
And other forms of life than ours,
What know we greater than the soul?
On God and Godlike men we build our trust.
Hush, the Dead March wails in the people's ears:
The dark crowd moves, and there are sobs and tears:
The black earth yawns: the mortal disappears;
Ashes to ashes, dust to dust;
He is gone who seem'd so great.—
Gone; but nothing can bereave him
Of the force he made his own
Being here, and we believe him
Something far advanced in State,
And that he wears a truer crown
Than any wreath that man can weave him.
Speak no more of his renown,
Lay your earthly fancies down,
And in the vast cathedral leave him.
God accept him, Christ receive him.

BRITAIN.

You ask me, why, tho' ill at ease,
    Within this region I subsist,
    Whose spirits falter in the mist,
And languish for the purple seas?

It is the land that freemen till,
    That sober-suited Freedom chose,
    The land, where girt with friends or foes
A man may speak the thing he will;

A land of settled government,
    A land of just and old renown,
    Where Freedom broadens slowly down
From precedent to precedent:

Where faction seldom gathers head,
    But by degrees to fullness wrought,
    The strength of some diffusive thought
Hath time and space to work and spread.

Should banded unions persecute
    Opinion, and induce a time
    When single thought is civil crime,
And individual freedom mute;

Tho' Power should make from land to land
    The name of Britain trebly great—
    Tho' every channel of the State
Should fill and choke with golden sand—

Yet waft me from the harbour-mouth,
    Wild wind! I seek a warmer sky,
    And I will see before I die
The palms and temples of the South.

FREEDOM.

Of old sat Freedom on the heights,
    The thunders breaking at her feet:
Above her shook the starry lights:
    She heard the torrents meet.

There in her place she did rejoice,
    Self-gather'd in her prophet-mind,
But fragments of her mighty voice
    Came rolling on the wind.

Then stept she down thro' town and field
    To mingle with the human race,
And part by part to men reveal'd
    The fullness of her face—

Grave mother of majestic works,
    From her isle-altar gazing down,
Who, God-like, grasps the triple forks,
    And, King-like, wears the crown:

Her open eyes desire the truth.
    The wisdom of a thousand years
Is in them.   May perpetual youth
    Keep dry their light from tears;

That her fair form may stand and shine,
    Make bright our days and light our dreams,
Turning to scorn with lips divine
    The falsehood of extremes!

FROM "MAUD."

1.

COME into the garden, Maud,
    For the black bat, night, has flown,
Come into the garden, Maud,
    I am here at the gate alone;
And the woodbine spices are wafted abroad,
    And the musk of the roses blown.

2.

For a breeze of morning moves,
    And the planet of Love is on high,
Beginning to faint in the light that she loves
    On a bed of daffodil sky,
To faint in the light of the sun she loves,
    To faint in his light, and to die.

10.

There has fallen a splendid tear
    From the passion-flower at the gate.
She is coming, my dove, my dear;
    She is coming, my life, my fate;

The red rose cries, 'She is near, she is near;'
   And the white rose weeps, 'She is late;'
The larkspur listens, 'I hear, I hear;'
   And the lily whispers, 'I wait.'

II.

She is coming, my own, my sweet;
   Were it ever so airy a tread,
My heart would hear her and beat,
   Were it earth in an earthy bed;
My dust would hear her and beat,
   Had I lain for a century dead;
Would start and tremble under her feet,
   And blossom in purple and red.

THE SAILOR BOY.

HE rose at dawn and, fired with hope,
   Shot o'er the seething harbour-bar,
And reach'd the ship and caught the rope,
   And whistled to the morning star.

And while he whistled long and loud
   He heard a fierce mermaiden cry,
' O boy, tho' thou art young and proud,
   I see the place where thou wilt lie.

' The sands and yeasty surges mix
   In caves about the dreary bay,
And on thy ribs the limpet sticks,
   And in thy heart the scrawl shall play.'

' Fool,' he answer'd, ' death is sure
   To those that stay and those that roam,
But I will nevermore endure
   To sit with empty hands at home.

'My mother clings about my neck,
    My sisters crying " stay for shame ;"
My father raves of death and wreck,
    They are all to blame, they are all to blame.

'God help me ! save I take my part
    Of danger on the roaring sea,
A devil rises in my heart,
    Far worse than any death to me.'

My life is full of weary days,
    But good things have not kept aloof,
Nor wandered into other ways:
    I have not lack'd thy mild reproof,
Nor golden largess of thy praise.

And now shake hands across the brink
    Of that deep grave to which I go :
Shake hands once more: I cannot sink
    So far—far down, but I shall know
    Thy voice, and answer from below.

Break, break, break,
  On thy cold gray stones, O Sea!
And I would that my tongue could utter
  The thoughts that arise in me.

O well for the fisherman's boy,
  That he shouts with his sister at play!
O well for the sailor lad,
  That he sings in his boat on the bay!

And the stately ships go on
  To their haven under the hill;
But O for the touch of a vanish'd hand,
  And the sound of a voice that is still!

Break, break, break,
  At the foot of thy crags, O Sea!
But the tender grace of a day that is dead
  Will never come back to me.

THE CHARGE OF THE LIGHT BRIGADE.

Oct 25, 1854.

I.

Half a league, half a league,
  Half a league onward,
All in the valley of Death
  Rode the six hundred.
"Forward, the Light Brigade!
"Charge for the guns!" he said:
Into the valley of Death
  Rode the six hundred.

2.

"Forward, the Light Brigade!"
Was there a man dismay'd?
Not tho' the soldier knew
  Some one had blunder'd:
Their's not to make reply,
Their's not to reason why,
Their's but to do and die:
Into the valley of Death
  Rode the six hundred.

o

3.

Cannon to right of them,
Cannon to left of them,
Cannon in front of them
   Volley'd and thunder'd;
Storm'd at with shot and shell,
Boldly they rode and well,
Into the jaws of Death,
Into the mouth of Hell
   Rode the six hundred.

4.

Flash'd all their sabres bare,
Flash'd as they turn'd in air,
Sabring the gunners there,
Charging an army, while
   All the world wonder'd:
Plunged in the battery-smoke
Right thro' the line they broke;
Cossack and Russian
Reel'd from the sabre-stroke
   Shatter'd and sunder'd.
Then they rode back, but not
   Not the six hundred.

5.

Cannon to right of them,
Cannon to left of them,
Cannon behind them
   Volley'd and thunder'd;
Storm'd at with shot and shell,
While horse and hero fell,
They that had fought so well
Came thro' the jaws of Death
Back from the mouth of Hell,
All that was left of them,
   Left of six hundred.

6.

When can their glory fade?
O the wild charge they made!
   All the world wonder'd.
Honour the charge they made!
Honour the Light Brigade,
   Noble six hundred!

THREE SONNETS TO A COQUETTE.

CARESS'D or chidden by the dainty hand,
   And singing airy trifles this or that,
Light Hope at Beauty's call would perch and stand,
   And run thro' every change of sharp and flat;
   And Fancy came and at her pillow sat,
When sleep had bound her in his rosy band,
   And chased away the still-recurring gnat,
And woke her with a lay from fairy land.
But now they live with Beauty less and less,
   For Hope is other Hope and wanders far,
     Nor cares to lisp in love's delicious creeds;
And Fancy watches in the wilderness,
   Poor Fancy sadder than a single star,
     That sets at twilight in a land of reeds.

2.

The form, the form alone is eloquent!
   A nobler yearning never broke her rest
   Than but to dance and sing, be gaily drest,
And win all eyes with all accomplishment:

Yet in the waltzing-circle as we went,
  My fancy made me for a moment blest
  To find my heart so near the beauteous breast
That once had power to rob it of content.
A moment came the tenderness of tears,
  The phantom of a wish that once could move,
    A ghost of passion that no smiles restore—
For ah ! the slight coquette, she cannot love,
And if you kiss'd her feet a thousand years,
    She still would take the praise, and care no more.

3.

Wan Sculptor weepest thou to take the cast
  Of those dead lineäments that near thee lie ?
O sorrowest thou, pale Painter, for the past,
  In painting some dead friend from memory ?
Weep on: beyond his object Love can last:
  His object lives: more cause to weep have I:
My tears, no tears of love, are flowing fast,
  No tears of love, but tears that Love can die.
I pledge her not in any cheerful cup,
  Nor care to sit beside her where she sits—
    Ah pity—hint it not in human tones,
But breathe it into earth and close it up
  With secret death for ever, in the pits
    Which some green Christmas crams with weary
      bones.

From "MAUD."

Go not, happy day,
　　From the shining fields,
Go not, happy day,
　　Till the maiden yields.
·Rosy is the West,
　　Rosy is the South,
Roses are her cheeks,
　　And a rose her mouth.
When the happy Yes
　　Falters from her lips,
Pass and blush the news
　　Over glowing ships;
Over blowing seas,
　　Over seas at rest,
Pass the happy news,
　　Blush it thro' the West;
Blush from West to East,
　　Blush from East to West,
Till the West is East,
　　Blush it thro' the West.
Rosy is the West,
　　Rosy is the South,
Roses are her cheeks,
　　And a rose her mouth.

A FAREWELL.

FLOW down, cold rivulet, to the sea,
    Thy tribute wave deliver:
No more by thee my steps shall be,
    For ever and for ever.

Flow, softly flow, by lawn and lea,
    A rivulet then a river:
No where by thee my steps shall be,
    For ever and for ever.

But here will sigh thine alder tree,
    And here thine aspen shiver;
And here by thee will hum the bee,
    For ever and for ever.

A thousand suns will stream on thee,
    A thousand moons will quiver;
But not by thee my steps shall be,
    For ever and for ever.

FROM THE "PRINCESS."

As thro' the land at eve we went,
   And pluck'd the ripen'd ears,
We fell out, my wife and I,
We fell out I know not why,
   And kiss'd again with tears.

And blessings on the falling out
   That all the more endears,
When we fall out with those we love
   And kiss again with tears !

For when we came where lies the child
   We lost in other years,
There above the little grave,
O there above the little grave,
   We kiss'd again with tears.

Sweet and low, sweet and low,
   Wind of the western sea,
Low, low, breathe and blow,
   Wind of the western sea !
Over the rolling waters go,
Come from the dying moon, and blow,
   Blow him again to me;
While my little one, while my pretty one, sleeps.

Sleep and rest, sleep and rest,
   Father will come to thee soon;
Rest, rest, on mother's breast,
   Father will come to thee soon;
Father will come to his babe in the nest,
Silver sails all out of the west
   Under the silver moon:
Sleep, my little one, sleep, my pretty one, sleep.

FROM THE SAME.

THE splendour falls on castle walls
And snowy summits old in story:
The long light shakes across the lakes,
And the wild cataract leaps in glory.
Blow, bugle, blow, set the wild echoes flying,
Blow, bugle; answer, echoes, dying, dying, dying.

O hark, O hear! how thin and clear,
And thinner, clearer, farther going!
O sweet and far from cliff and scar
The horns of Elfland faintly blowing!
Blow, let us hear the purple glens replying:
Blow, bugle; answer, echoes, dying, dying, dying.

O love, they die in yon rich sky,
They faint on hill or field or river:
Our echoes roll from soul to soul,
And grow for ever and for ever.
Blow, bugle, blow, set the wild echoes flying,
And answer, echoes, answer, dying, dying, dying.

From the Same.

"Tears, idle tears, I know not what they mean,
Tears from the depth of some divine despair
Rise in the heart, and gather to the eyes,
In looking on the happy Autumn-fields,
And thinking of the days that are no more.

"Fresh as the first beam glittering on a sail,
That brings our friends up from the underworld,
Sad as the last which reddens over one
That sinks with all we love below the verge;
So sad, so fresh, the days that are no more.

"Ah, sad and strange as in dark summer dawns
The earliest pipe of half-awaken'd birds
To dying ears, when unto dying eyes
The casement slowly grows a glimmering square;
So sad, so strange, the days that are no more.

" Dear as remember'd kisses after death,
And sweet as those by hopeless fancy feign'd
On lips that are for others; deep as love,
Deep as first love, and wild with all regret;
O Death in Life, the days that are no more."

'O SWALLOW, Swallow, flying, flying South,
Fly to her, and fall upon her gilded eaves,
And tell her, tell her, what I tell to thee.

'O tell her, Swallow, thou that knowest each,
That bright and fierce and fickle is the South,
And dark and true and tender is the North.

'O Swallow, Swallow, if I could follow, and light
Upon her lattice, I would pipe and trill,
And cheep and twitter twenty million loves.

'O were I thou that she might take me in,
And lay me on her bosom, and her heart
Would rock the snowy cradle till I died.

'Why lingereth she to clothe her heart with love,
Delaying as the tender ash delays
To clothe herself, when all the woods are green?

' O tell her, Swallow, that thy brood is flown:
Say to her, I do but wanton in the South,
But in the North long since my nest is made.

' O tell her, brief is life but love is long,
And brief the sun of summer in the North,
And brief the moon of beauty in the South.

' O Swallow, flying from the golden woods,
Fly to her, and pipe and woo her, and make her mine.
And tell her, tell her, that I follow thee.'

SONG.

LADY, let the rolling drums
Beat to battle where thy warrior stands:
Now thy face across his fancy comes,
   And gives the battle to his hands.

Lady, let the trumpets blow,
Clasp thy little babes about thy knee:
Now their warrior father meets the foe,
   And strikes him dead for thine and thee.

SONG.

HOME they brought him slain with spears.
   They brought him home at even-fall:
All alone she sits and hears
   Echoes in his empty hall,
      Sounding on the morrow.

The Sun peep'd in from open field,
   The boy began to leap and prance,
   Rode upon his father's lance,
Beat upon his father's shield—
      "O hush, my joy, my sorrow."

From the "*PRINCESS*."

' Home they brought her warrior dead :
   She nor swoon'd, nor utter'd cry :
.All her maidens, watching, said,
   ' She must weep or she will die.'

Then they praised him, soft and low,
   Call'd him worthy to be loved,
Truest friend and noblest foe ;
   Yet she neither spoke nor moved.

Stole a maiden from her place,
   Lightly to the warrior stept,
Took the face-cloth from the face ;
   Yet she neither moved nor wept.

Rose a nurse of ninety years,
   And set his child upon her knee—
Like summer tempest came her tears—
   ' O my child, I live for thee.'

Ask me no more : the moon may draw the sea ;
   The cloud may stoop from heaven and take the
      shape,
   With fold to fold, of mountain or of cape ;
But O too fond, when have I answer'd thee ?
       Ask me no more.

Ask me no more : what answer should I give ?
   I love not hollow cheek or faded eye :
   Yet, O my friend, I will not have thee die !
Ask me no more, lest I should bid thee live ;
       Ask me no more.

Ask me no more : thy fate and mine are seal'd :
   I strove against the stream and all in vain :
   Let the great river take me to the main :
No more, dear love, for at a touch I yield ;
       Ask me no more.

P

From the Same.

' Now sleeps the crimson petal, now the white ;
Nor waves the cypress in the palace walk ;
Nor winks the gold fin in the porphyry font :
The fire-fly wakens : waken thou with me.

Now droops the milkwhite peacock like a ghost,
And like a ghost she glimmers on to me.

Now lies the Earth all Danaë to the stars,
And all thy heart lies open unto me.

Now slides the silent meteor on, and leaves
A shining furrow, as thy thoughts in me.

Now folds the lily all her sweetness up,
And slips into the bosom of the lake :
So fold thyself, my dearest, thou, and slip
Into my bosom and be lost in me.'

' COME down, O maid, from yonder mountain
  height :
What pleasure lives in height (the Shepherd sang)
In height and cold, the splendour of the hills?
But cease to move so near the Heavens, and cease
To glide a sunbeam by the blasted Pine,
To sit a star upon the sparkling spire ;
And come, for Love is of the valley, come,
For Love is of the valley, come thou down
And find him ; by the happy threshold, he,
Or hand in hand with Plenty in the maize,
Or red with spirted purple of the vats,
Or foxlike in the vine ; nor cares to walk
With Death and Morning on the silver horns,
Nor wilt thou snare him in the white ravine,
Nor find him dropt upon the firths of ice,
That huddling slant in furrow-cloven falls
To roll the torrent out of dusky doors :
But follow ; let the torrent dance thee down
To find him in the valley ; let the wild

Lean-headed Eagles yelp alone, and leave
The monstrous ledges there to slope, and spill
Their thousand wreaths of dangling water-smoke,
That like a broken purpose waste in air :
So waste not thou ; but come ; for all the vales
Await thee ; azure pillars of the hearth
Arise to thee ; the children call, and I
Thy shepherd pipe, and sweet is every sound,
Sweeter thy voice, but every sound is sweet ;
Myriads of rivulets hurrying thro' the lawn,
The moan of doves in immemorial elms,
And murmuring of innumerable bees.'

CRADLE SONG.

WHAT does little birdie say
In her nest at peep of day?
Let me fly, says little birdie,
Mother, let me fly away.
Birdie, rest a little longer,
Till the little wings are stronger.
So she rests a little longer,
Then she flies away.

What does little baby say,
In her bed at peep of day?
Baby says, like little birdie,
Let me rise and fly away.
Baby, sleep a little longer,
Till the little limbs are stronger.
If she sleeps a little longer,
Baby too shall fly away.

From the "*IDYLLS OF THE KING.*"

ENID'S SONG.

'Turn, Fortune, turn thy wheel and lower the proud;
Turn thy wild wheel thro' sunshine, storm, and cloud;
Thy wheel and thee we neither love nor hate.

'Turn, Fortune, turn thy wheel with smile or frown;
With that wild wheel we go not up or down;
Our hoard is little, but our hearts are great.

'Smile and we smile, the lords of many lands;
Frown and we smile, the lords of our own hands;
For man is man and master of his fate.

'Turn, turn thy wheel above the staring crowd;
Thy wheel and thou are shadows in the cloud;
Thy wheel and thee we neither love nor hate.'

VIVIEN'S SONG.

"In Love, if Love be Love, if Love be ours,
Faith and unfaith can ne'er be equal powers:
Unfaith in aught is want of faith in all.

" It is the little rift within the lute,
That by and by will make the music mute,
And ever widening slowly silence all.

"The little rift within the lover's lute,
Or little pitted speck in garner'd fruit,
That rotting inward slowly moulders all.

" It is not worth the keeping: let it go:
But shall it? answer, darling, answer, no.
And trust me not at all or all in all."

ELAINE'S SONG.

"SWEET is true love tho' given in vain, in vain;
And sweet is death who puts an end to pain:
I know not which is sweeter, no, not I.

"Love, art thou sweet? then bitter death must be:
Love, thou art bitter; sweet is death to me.
O Love, if death be sweeter, let me die.

"Sweet love, that seems not made to fade away,
Sweet death, that seems to make us loveless clay,
I know not which is sweeter, no, not I.

"I fain would follow love, if that could be;
I needs must follow death, who calls for me;
Call and I follow, I follow! let me die."

From the "*DAY DREAM.*"

THE DEPARTURE.

1.

AND on her lover's arm she leant,
 And round her waist she felt it fold,
And far across the hills they went
 In that new world which is the old:
Across the hills, and far away
 Beyond their utmost purple rim,
And deep into the dying day
 The happy princess follow'd him.

2.

"I'd sleep another hundred years,
 O love, for such another kiss;"
"O wake for ever, love," she hears,
 "O love, 'twas such as this and this."

And o'er them many a sliding star,
   And many a merry wind was borne,
And, stream'd thro' many a golden bar,
   The twilight melted into morn.

3.

"O eyes long laid in happy sleep !"
   "O happy sleep, that lightly fled !"
"O happy kiss, that woke thy sleep !"
   "O love, thy kiss would wake the dead !"
And o'er them many a flowing range
   Of vapour buoy'd the crescent-bark,
And, rapt thro' many a rosy change,
   The twilight died into the dark.

4.

"A hundred summers ! can it be ?
   And whither goest thou, tell me where ?"
"O seek my father's court with me,
   For there are greater wonders there."
And o'er the hills, and far away
   Beyond their utmost purple rim,
Beyond the night, across the day,
   Thro' all the world she follow'd him.

WILL.

I.

O WELL for him whose will is strong!
He suffers, but he will not suffer long;
He suffers, but he cannot suffer wrong:
For him nor moves the loud world's random mock,
Nor all Calamity's hugest waves confound,
Who seems a promontory of rock,
That, compass'd round with turbulent sound,
In middle ocean meets the surging shock,
Tempest-buffeted, citadel-crown'd.

2.

But ill for him who, bettering not with time,
Corrupts the strength of heaven-descended Will,
And ever weaker grows thro' acted crime,
Or seeming-genial venial fault,
Recurring and suggesting still!
He seems as one whose footsteps halt,
Toiling in immeasurable sand,
And o'er a weary sultry land,
Far beneath a blazing vault,
Sown in a wrinkle of the monstrous hill,
The city sparkles like a grain of salt.

ON A MOURNER.

Nature, so far as in her lies,
  Imitates God, and turns her face
To every land beneath the skies,
  Counts nothing that she meets with base,
  But lives and loves in every place;

2.

Fills out the homely quickset-screens,
  And makes the purple lilac ripe,
Steps from her airy hill, and greens
  The swamp, where hums the dropping snipe,
  With moss and braided marish-pipe;

3.

And on thy heart a finger lays,
  Saying, ' beat quicker, for the time
Is pleasant, and the woods and ways
  Are pleasant, and the beech and lime
  Put forth and feel a gladder clime.'

4.

And murmurs of a deeper voice,
   Going before to some far shrine,
Teach that sick heart the stronger choice,
   Till all thy life one way incline
   With one wide will that closes thine.

5.

And when the zoning eve has died
   Where yon dark valleys wind forlorn,
Come Hope and Memory, spouse and bride,
   From out the borders of the morn,
   With that fair child betwixt them born.

6.

And when no mortal motion jars
   The blackness round the tombing sod,
Thro' silence and the trembling stars
   Comes Faith from tracts no feet have trod,
   And Virtue, like a household god

7.

Promising empire; such as those
   That once at dead of night did greet
Troy's wandering prince, so that he rose
   With sacrifice, while all the fleet
   Had rest by stony hills of Crete.

THE SEA-FAIRIES.

SLOW sail'd the weary mariners and saw,
Betwixt the green brink and the running foam,
Sweet faces, rounded arms, and bosoms prest
To little harps of gold; and while they mused,
Whispering to each other half in fear,
Shrill music reach'd them on the middle sea.

Whither away, whither away, whither away? fly no
　　more.
Whither away from the high green field, and the happy
　　blossoming shore?
Day and night to the billow the fountain calls;
Down shower the gambolling waterfalls
From wandering over the lea:
Out of the live-green heart of the dells
They freshen the silvery-crimson shells,
And thick with white bells the clover-hill swells
High over the full-toned sea:
O hither, come hither and furl your sails,
Come hither to me and to me:

Hither, come hither and frolic and play;
Here it is only the mew that wails;
We will sing to you all the day:
Mariner, mariner, furl your sails,
For here are the blissful downs and dales,
And merrily merrily carol the gales,
And the spangle dances in bight and bay,
And the rainbow forms and flies on the land
Over the islands free;
And the rainbow lives in the curve of the sand;
Hither, come hither and see;
And the rainbow hangs on the poising wave,
And sweet is the colour of cove and cave,
And sweet shall your welcome be:
O hither, come hither, and be our lords,
For merry brides are we:
We will kiss sweet kisses, and speak sweet words:
O listen, listen, your eyes shall glisten
With pleasure and love and jubilee:
O listen, listen, your eyes shall glisten
When the sharp clear twang of the golden chords
Runs up the ridged sea.
Who can light on as happy a shore
All the world o'er, all the world o'er?
Whither away? listen and stay: mariner, mariner, fly
 no more.

THE POET'S SONG.

THE rain had fallen, the Poet arose,
   He pass'd by the town and out of the street,
A light wind blew from the gates of the sun,
   And waves of shadow went over the wheat,
And he sat him down in a lonely place,
   And chanted a melody loud and sweet,
That made the wild-swan pause in her cloud,
   And the lark drop down at his feet.

The swallow stopt as he hunted the bee,
   The snake slipt under a spray,
The wild hawk stood with the down on his beak,
   And stared, with his foot on the prey,
And the nightingale thought, "I have sung many songs,
   But never a one so gay,
For he sings of what the world will be
   When the years have died away."

FROM THE "*IDYLLS OF THE KING.*"

GUINEVERE.

QUEEN GUINEVERE had fled the court, and sat
There in the holy house at Almesbury
Weeping, none with her save a little maid,
A novice: one low light betwixt them burn'd
Blurr'd by the creeping mist, for all abroad,
Beneath a moon unseen albeit at full,
The white mist, like a face-cloth to the face,
Clung to the dead earth, and the land was still.

For hither had she fled, her cause of flight
Sir Modred; he the nearest to the King,
His nephew, ever like a subtle beast
Lay couchant with his eyes upon the throne,
Ready to spring, waiting a chance: for this,
He chill'd the popular praises of the King
With silent smiles of slow disparagement;
And tamper'd with the Lords of the White Horse,
Heathen, the brood by Hengist left; and sought

Q

To make disruption in the Table Round
Of Arthur, and to splinter it into feuds
Serving his traitorous end; and all his aims
Were sharpen'd by strong hate for Lancelot.

For thus it chanced one morn when all the court,
Green-suited, but with plumes that mock'd the may,
Had been, their wont, a-maying and return'd,
That Modred still in green, all ear and eye,
Climb'd to the high top of the garden-wall
To spy some secret scandal if he might,
And saw the Queen who sat betwixt her best
Enid, and lissome Vivien, of her court
The wiliest and the worst; and more than this
He saw not, for Sir Lancelot passing by
Spied where he couch'd, and as the gardener's hand
Picks from the colewort a green caterpillar,
So from the high wall and the flowering grove
Of grasses Lancelot pluck'd him by the heel,
And cast him as a worm upon the way;   .
But when he knew the Prince tho' marr'd with dust,
He, reverencing king's blood in a bad man,
Made such excuses as he might, and these
Full knightly without scorn; for in those days
No knight of Arthur's noblest dealt in scorn;
But, if a man were halt or hunch'd, in him

By those whom God had made full-limb'd and tall,
Scorn was allow'd as part of his defect,
And he was answer'd softly by the King
And all his Table.   So Sir Lancelot holp
To raise the Prince, who rising twice or thrice
Full sharply smote his knees, and smiled, and went:
But, ever after, the small violence done
Rankled in him and ruffled all his heart,
As the sharp wind that ruffles all day long
A little bitter pool about a stone
On the bare coast.

                  But when Sir Lancelot told
This matter to the Queen, at first she laugh'd
Lightly, to think of Modred's dusty fall,
Then shudder'd, as the village wife who cries
' I shudder, some one steps across my grave; '
Then laugh'd again, but faintlier, for indeed
She half-foresaw that he, the subtle beast,
Would track her guilt until he found, and hers
Would be for evermore a name of scorn.
Henceforward rarely could she front in Hall,
Or elsewhere, Modred's narrow foxy face,
Heart-hiding smile, and gray persistent eye:
Henceforward too, the Powers that tend the soul,
To help it from the death that cannot die,
And save it even in extremes, began

To vex and plague her.   Many a time for hours,
Beside the placid breathings of the King,
In the dead night, grim faces came and went
Before her, or a vague spiritual fear—
Like to some doubtful noise of creaking doors,
Heard by the watcher in a haunted house,
That keeps the rust of murder on the walls—
Held her awake: or if she slept, she dream'd
An awful dream; for then she seem'd to stand
On some vast plain before a setting sun,
And from the sun there swiftly made at her
A ghastly something, and its shadow flew
Before it, till it touch'd her, and she turn'd—
When lo ! her own, that broadening from her feet,
And blackening, swallow'd all the land, and in it
Far cities burnt, and with a cry she woke.
And all this trouble did not pass but grew;
Till ev'n the clear face of the guileless King,
And trustful courtesies of household life,
Became her bane; and at the last she said,
' O Lancelot, get thee hence to thine own land,
For if thou tarry we shall meet again,
And if we meet again, some evil chance
Will make the smouldering scandal break and blaze
Before the people, and our lord the King.'
And Lancelot ever promised, but remain'd,

And still they met and met. Again she said,
' O Lancelot, if thou love me get thee hence.'
And then they were agreed upon a night
(When the good King should not be there) to meet
And part for ever. Passion-pale they met
And greeted: hands in hands, and eye to eye,
Low on the border of her couch they sat
Stammering and staring: it was their last hour,
A madness of farewells. And Modred brought
His creatures to the basement of the tower
For testimony; and crying with full voice
' Traitor, come out, ye are trapt at last,' aroused
Lancelot, who rushing outward lionlike
Leapt on him, and hurl'd him headlong, and he fell
Stunn'd, and his creatures took and bare him off
And all was still: then she, 'the end is come
And I am shamed for ever;' and he said
' Mine be the shame; mine was the sin: but rise,
And fly to my strong castle overseas:
There will I hide thee, till my life shall end,
There hold thee with my life against the world.'
She answer'd 'Lancelot, wilt thou hold me so?
Nay friend, for we have taken our farewells.
Would God, that thou could'st hide me from myself!
Mine is the shame, for I was wife, and thou
Unwedded: yet rise now, and let us fly,

For I will draw me into sanctuary,
And bide my doom.'   So Lancelot got her horse,
Set her thereon, and mounted on his own,
And then they rode to the divided way,
There kiss'd, and parted weeping: for he past,
Love-loyal to the least wish of the Queen,
Back to his land; but she to Almesbury
Fled all night long by glimmering waste and weald,
And heard the Spirits of the waste and weald
Moan as she fled, or thought she heard them moan:
And in herself she moan'd 'too late, too late!'
Till in the cold wind that foreruns the morn,
A blot in heaven, the Raven, flying high,
Croak'd, and she thought 'he spies a field of death;
For now the Heathen of the Northern Sea,
Lured by the crimes and frailties of the court,
Begin to slay the folk, and spoil the land.'

  And when she came to Almesbury she spake
There to the nuns, and said, 'mine enemies
Pursue me, but, O peaceful Sisterhood,
Receive, and yield me sanctuary, nor ask
Her name, to whom ye yield it, till her time
To tell you:' and her beauty, grace and power,
Wrought as a charm upon them, and they spared
To ask it.

So the stately Queen abode
For many a week, unknown, among the nuns;
Nor with them mix'd, nor told her name, nor sought,
Wrapt in her grief, for housel or for shrift,
But communed only with the little maid,
Who pleased her with a babbling heedlessness
Which often lured her from herself; but now,
This night, a rumour wildly blown about
Came, that Sir Modred had usurped the realm,
And leagued him with the heathen, while the King
Was waging war on Lancelot: then she thought,
'With what a hate the people and the King
Must hate me,' and bow'd down upon her hands
Silent, until the little maid, who brook'd
No silence, brake it, uttering 'late ! so late !
What hour, I wonder, now ?' and when she drew
No answer, by and by began to hum
An air the nuns had taught her; 'late, so late !'
Which when she heard, the Queen look'd up, and said,
'O maiden, if indeed you list to sing,
Sing, and unbind my heart that I may weep.'
Whereat full willingly sang the little maid.

"Late, late, so late ! and dark the night and chill !
Late, late, so late ! but we can enter still.
Too late, too late ! ye cannot enter now.

"No light had we: for that we do repent;
And learning this, the bridegroom will relent.
Too late, too late! ye cannot enter now.

"No light: so late! and dark and chill the night!
O let us in, that we may find the light!
Too late, too late: ye cannot enter now.

"Have we not heard the bridegroom is so sweet?
O let us in, tho' late, to kiss his feet!
No, no, too late! ye cannot enter now."

So sang the novice, while full passionately,
Her head upon her hands, remembering
Her thought when first she came, wept the sad Queen.
Then said the little novice prattling to her.

'O pray you, noble lady, weep no more;
But let my words, the words of one so small,
Who knowing nothing knows but to obey,
And if I do not there is penance given—
Comfort your sorrows; for they do not flow
From evil done; right sure am I of that,
Who see your tender grace and stateliness.
But weigh your sorrows with our lord the King's,
And weighing find them less; for gone is he

To wage grim war against Sir Lancelot there,
Round that strong castle where he holds the Queen;
And Modred whom he left in charge óf all,
The traitor—Ah sweet lady, the King's grief
For his own self, and his own Queen, and realm,
Must needs be thrice as great as any of ours.
For me, I thank the saints, I am not great.
For if there ever come a grief to me
I cry my cry in silence, and have done:
None knows it, and my tears have brought me good:
But even were the griefs of little ones
As great as those of great ones, yet this grief
Is added to the griefs the great must bear,
That howsoever much they may desire
Silence, they cannot weep behind a cloud:
As even here they talk at Almesbury
About the good King and his wicked Queen,
And were I such a King with such a Queen,
Well might I wish to veil her wickedness,
But were I such a King, it could not be.'

   Then to her own sad heart mutter'd the Queen.
'Will the child kill me with her innocent talk?'
But openly she answer'd 'must not I,
If this false traitor have displaced his lord,
Grieve with the common grief of all the realm?'

'Yea,' said the maid, 'this is all woman's grief,
That *she* is woman, whose disloyal life
Hath wrought confusion in the Table Round
Which good King Arthur founded, years ago,
With signs and miracles and wonders, there
At Camelot, ere the coming of the Queen.'

Then thought the Queen within herself again;
'Will the child kill me with her foolish prate?'
But openly she spake and said to her;
'O little maid, shut in by nunnery walls,
What canst thou know of Kings and Tables Round,
Or what of signs and wonders, but the signs
And simple miracles of thy nunnery?'

To whom the little novice garrulously.
'Yea, but I know: the land was full of signs
And wonders ere the coming of the Queen.
So said my father, and himself was knight
Of the great Table—at the founding of it;
And rode thereto from Lyonnesse, and he said
That as he rode, an hour or maybe twain
After the sunset, down the coast, he heard
Strange music, and he paused and turning—there
All down the lonely coast of Lyonnesse,
Each with a beacon-star upon his head,

And with a wild sea-light about his feet,
He saw them—headland after headland flame
Far on into the rich heart of the west:
And in the light the white mermaiden swam,
And strong man-breasted things stood from the sea,
And sent a deep sea-voice thro' all the land,
To which the little elves of chasm and cleft
Made answer, sounding like a distant horn.
So said my father—yea, and furthermore,
Next morning, while he past the dim-lit woods,
Himself beheld three spirits mad with joy
Come dashing down on a tall wayside flower,
That shook beneath them, as the thistle shakes
When three gray linnets wrangle for the seed:
And still at evenings on before his horse
The flickering fairy-circle wheel'd and broke
Flying, and link'd again, and wheel'd and broke
Flying, for all the land was full of life.
And when at last he came to Camelot,
A wreath of airy dancers hand-in-hand
Swung round the lighted lantern of the hall;
And in the hall itself was such a feast
As never man had dream'd; for every knight
Had whatsoever meat he long'd for served
By hands unseen; and even as he said
Down in the cellars merry bloated things

Shoulder'd the spigot, straddling on the butts
While the wine ran : so glad were spirits and men
Before the coming of the sinful Queen.'

    Then spake the Queen and somewhat bitterly.
' Were they so glad? ill prophets were they all,
Spirits and men : could none of them foresee,
Not even thy wise father with his signs
And wonders, what has fall'n upon the realm?'

    To whom the novice garrulously again.
' Yea, one, a bard ; of whom my father said,
Full many a noble war-song had he sung,
Ev'n in the presence of an enemy's fleet,
Between the steep cliff and the coming wave ;
And many a mystic lay of life and death
Had chanted on the smoky mountain-tops,
When round him bent the spirits of the hills
With all their dewy hair blown back like flame :
So said my father—and that night the bard
Sang Arthur's glorious wars, and sang the King
As well-nigh more than man, and rail'd at those
Who call'd him the false son of Gorloïs :
For there was no man knew from whence he came ;
But after tempest, when the long wave broke
All down the thundering shores of Bude and Bos,

There came a day as still as heaven, and then
They found a naked child upon the sands
Of dark Tintagil by the Cornish sea;
And that was Arthur; and they foster'd him
Till he by miracle was approven king:
And that his grave should be a mystery
From all men, like his birth; and could he find
A woman in her womanhood as great
As he was in his manhood, then, he sang,
The twain together well might change the world.
But even in the middle of his song
He falter'd, and his hand fell from the harp,
And pale he turn'd, and reel'd, and would have fall'n,
But that they stay'd him up; nor would he tell
His vision; but what doubt that he foresaw
This evil work of Lancelot and the Queen?'

    Then thought the Queen 'lo! they have set her on,
Our simple-seeming Abbess and her nuns,
To play upon me,' and bow'd her head nor spake.
Whereat the novice crying, with clasp'd hands,
Shame on her own garrulity garrulously,
Said the good nuns would check her gadding tongue
Full often, 'and, sweet lady, if I seem
To vex an ear too sad to listen to me,
Unmannerly, with prattling and the tales

Which my good father told, check me too :
Nor let me shame my father's memory, one
Of noblest manners, tho' himself would say
Sir Lancelot had the noblest ; and he died,
Kill'd in a tilt, come next, five summers back,
And left me ; but of others who remain,
And of the two first-famed for courtesy—
And pray you check me if I ask amiss—
But pray you, which had noblest, while you moved
Among them, Lancelot or our lord the King?'

  Then the pale Queen look'd up and answer'd her.
'Sir Lancelot, as became a noble knight,
Was gracious to all ladies, and the same
In open battle or the tilting-field
Forbore his own advantage, and the King
In open battle or the tilting-field
Forbore his own advantage, and these two
Were the most nobly-mannered men of all ;
For manners are not idle, but the fruit
Of loyal nature, and of noble mind.'

  'Yea,' said the maid, 'be manners such fair fruit?
Then Lancelot's needs must be a thousand-fold
Less noble, being, as all rumour runs,
The most disloyal friend in all the world.'

To which a mournful answer made the Queen.
'O closed about by narrowing nunnery-walls,
What knowest thou of the world, and all its lights
And shadows, all the wealth and all the woe?
If ever Lancelot, that most noble knight,
Were for one hour less noble than himself,
Pray for him that he scape the doom of fire,
And weep for her, who drew him to his doom.'

'Yea,' said the little novice, 'I pray for both;
But I should all as soon believe that his,
Sir Lancelot's, were as noble as the King's,
As I could think, sweet lady, yours would be
Such as they are, were you the sinful Queen.'

So she, like many another babbler, hurt
Whom she would soothe, and harm'd where she would
        heal;
For here a sudden flush of wrathful heat
Fired all the pale face of the Queen, who cried,
'Such as thou art be never maiden more
For ever! thou their tool, set on to plague
And play upon, and harry me, petty spy
And traitress.'   When that storm of anger brake
From Guinevere, aghast the maiden rose,
White as her veil, and stood before the Queen

As tremulously as foam upon the beach
Stands in a wind, ready to break and fly,
And when the Queen had added 'get thee hence'
Fled frighted.   Then that other left alone
Sigh'd, and began to gather heart again,
Saying in herself 'the simple, fearful child
Meant nothing, but my own too-fearful guilt
Simpler than any child, betrays itself.
But help me, heaven, for surely I repent.
For what is true repentance but in thought—
Not ev'n in inmost thought to think again
The sins that made the past so pleasant to us:
And I have sworn never to see him more,
To see him more.'
                    And ev'n in saying this,
Her memory from old habit of the mind
Went slipping back upon the golden days
In which she saw him first, when Lancelot came,
Reputed the best knight and goodliest man,
Ambassador, to lead her to his lord
Arthur, and led her forth, and far ahead
Of his and her retinue moving, they,
Rapt in sweet talk or lively, all on love
And sport and tilts and pleasure, (for the time
Was maytime, and as yet no sin was dream'd,)
Rode under groves that look'd a paradise

Of blossom, over sheets of hyacinth
That seem'd the heavens upbreaking thro' the earth,
And on from hill to hill, and every day
Beheld at noon in some delicious dale
The silk pavilions of King Arthur raised
For brief repast or afternoon repose
By couriers gone before; and on again,
Till yet once more ere set of sun they saw
The Dragon of the great Pendragonship,
That crown'd the state pavilion of the King,
Blaze by the rushing brook or silent well.

But when the Queen immersed in such a trance,
And moving thro' the past unconsciously,
Came to that point, when first she saw the King
Ride toward her from the city, sigh'd to find
Her journey done, glanced at him, thought him cold,
High, self-contain'd, and passionless, not like him,
' Not like my Lancelot'—while she brooded thus
And grew half-guilty in her thoughts again,
There rode an armed warrior to the doors.
A murmuring whisper thro' the nunnery ran,
Then on a sudden a cry, 'the King.' She sat
Stiff-stricken, listening; but when armed feet
Thro' the long gallery from the outer doors
Rang coming, prone from off her seat she fell,

R

And grovell'd with her face against the floor:
There with her milkwhite arms and shadowy hair
She made her face a darkness from the King:
And in the darkness heard his armed feet
Pause by her; then came silence, then a voice,
Monotonous and hollow like a Ghost's
Denouncing judgment, but tho' changed the King's.

   'Liest thou here so low, the child of one
I honour'd, happy, dead before thy shame?
Well is it that no child is born of thee.
The children born of thee are sword and fire,.
Red ruin, and the breaking up of laws,
The craft of kindred and the Godless hosts
Of heathen swarming o'er the Northern Sea.
Whom I, while yet Sir Lancelot, my right arm,
The mightiest of my knights, abode with me,
Have everywhere about this land of Christ
In twelve great battles ruining overthrown.
And knowest thou now from whence I come—from him,
From waging bitter war with him: and he,
That did not shun to smite me in worse way,
Had yet that grace of courtesy in him left,
He spared to lift his hand against the King
Who made him knight: but many a knight was slain;
And many more, and all his kith and kin

Clave to him, and abode in his own land.
And many more when Modred raised revolt,
Forgetful of their troth and fealty, clave
To Modred, and a remnant stays with me.
And of this remnant will I leave a part,
True men who love me still, for whom I live,
To guard thee in the wild hour coming on,
Lest but a hair of this low head be harm'd.
Fear not: thou shalt be guarded till my death.
Howbeit I know, if ancient prophecies
Have err'd not, that I march to meet my doom.
Thou hast not made my life so sweet to me,
That I the King should greatly care to live;
For thou hast spoilt the purpose of my life.
Bear with me for the last time while I show,
Ev'n for thy sake, the sin which thou hast sinn'd.
For when the Roman left us, and their law
Relax'd its hold upon us, and the ways
Were fill'd with rapine, here and there a deed
Of prowess done redress'd a random wrong.
But I was first of all the kings who drew
The knighthood-errant of this realm and all
The realms together under me, their Head,
In that fair order of my Table Round,
A glorious company, the flower of men,
To serve as model for the mighty world,

And be the fair beginning of a time.
I made them lay their hands in mine and swear
To reverence the King, as if he were
Their conscience, and their conscience as their King,
To break the heathen and uphold the Christ,
To ride abroad redressing human wrongs,
To speak no slander, no, nor listen to it,
To lead sweet lives in purest chastity,
To love one maiden only, cleave to her,
And worship her by years of noble deeds,
Until they won her; for indeed I knew
Of no more subtle master under heaven
Than is the maiden passion for a maid,
Not only to keep down the base in man,
But teach high thought, and amiable words
And courtliness, and the desire of fame,
And love of truth, and all that makes a man.
And all this throve until I wedded thee !
Believing "lo mine helpmate, one to feel
My purpose and rejoicing in my joy."
Then came thy shameful sin with Lancelot;
Then came the sin of Tristram and Isolt;
Then others, following these my mightiest knights,
And drawing foul ensample from fair names,
Sinn'd also, till the loathsome opposite
Of all my heart had destined did obtain,

And all thro' thee ! so that this life of mine
I guard as God's high gift from scathe and wrong,
Not greatly care to lose; but rather think
How sad it were for Arthur, should he live,
To sit once more within his lonely hall,
And miss the wonted number of my knights,
And miss to hear high talk of noble deeds
As in the golden days before thy sin.
For which of us, who might be left, could speak
Of the pure heart, nor seem to glance at thee ?
And in thy bowers of Camelot or of Usk
Thy shadow still would glide from room to room,
And I should evermore be vext with thee
In hanging robe or vacant ornament,
Or ghostly footfall echoing on the stair.
For think not, tho' thou would'st not love thy lord,
Thy lord has wholly lost his love for thee.
I am not made of so slight elements.
Yet must I leave thee, woman, to thy shame.
I hold that man the worst of public foes
Who either for his own or children's sake,
To save his blood from scandal, lets the wife
Whom he knows false, abide and rule the house:
For being thro' his cowardice allow'd
Her station, taken everywhere for pure,
She like a new disease, unknown to men,

Creeps, no precaution used, among the crowd,
Makes wicked lightnings of her eyes, and saps
The fealty of our friends, and stirs the pulse
With devil's leaps, and poisons half the young.
Worst of the worst were that man he that reigns!
Better the King's waste hearth and aching heart
Than thou reseated in thy place of light,
The mockery of my people, and their bane.'

 He paused, and in the pause she crept an inch
Nearer, and laid her hands about his feet.
Far off a solitary trumpet blew.
Then waiting by the doors the warhorse neigh'd
As at a friend's voice, and he spake again.

 'Yet think not that I come to urge thy crimes,
I did not come to curse thee, Guinevere,
I, whose vast pity almost makes me die
To see thee, laying there thy golden head,
My pride in happier summers, at my feet.
The wrath which forced my thoughts on that fierce law,
The doom of treason and the flaming death,
(When first I learnt thee hidden here) is past.
The pang—which while I weigh'd thy heart with one
Too wholly true to dream untruth in thee,
Made my tears burn—is also past, in part.

And all is past, the sin is sinn'd, and I,
Lo ! I forgive thee, as Eternal God
Forgives : do thou for thine own soul the rest.
But how to take last leave of all I loved ?
O golden hair, with which I used to play
Not knowing ! O imperial-moulded form,
And beauty such as never woman wore,
Until it came a kingdom's curse with thee—
I cannot touch thy lips, they are not mine,
But Lancelot's : nay, they never were the. King's.
I cannot take thy hand ; that too is flesh,
And in the flesh thou hast sinn'd ; and mine own flesh,
Here looking down on thine polluted, cries
" I loathe thee : " yet not less, O Guineyere,
For I was ever virgin save for thee,
My love thro' flesh hath wrought into my life
So far, that my doom is, I love thee still.
Let no man dream but that I love thee still.
Perchance, and so thou purify thy soul,
And so thou lean on our fair father Christ,
Hereafter in that world where all are pure
We two may meet before high God, and thou
Wilt spring to me, and claim me thine, and know
I am thine husband—not a smaller soul,
Nor Lancelot, nor another. Leave me that,
I charge thee, my last hope. Now must I hence.

Thro' the thick night I hear the trumpet blow :
They summon me their King to lead mine hosts
Far down to that great battle in the west,
Where I must strike against my sister's son,
Leagued with the lords of the White Horse and knights
Once mine, and strike him dead, and meet myself
Death, or I know not what mysterious doom.
And thou remaining here wilt learn the event;
But hither shall I never come again,
Never lie by thy side, see thee no more,
Farewell !'
             And while she grovell'd at his feet,
She felt the King's breath wander o'er her neck,
And, in the darkness o'er her fallen head,
Perceived the waving of his hands that blest.

    Then, listening till those armed steps were gone,
Rose the pale Queen, and in her anguish found
The casement : ' peradventure ' so she thought,
' If I might see his face, and not be seen.'
And lo, he sat on horseback at the door !
And near him the sad nuns with each a light
Stood, and he gave them charge about the Queen,
To guard and foster her for evermore.
And while he spake to these his helm was lower'd,
To which for crest the golden dragon clung

Of Britain ; so she did not see the face,
Which then was as an angel's, but she saw,
Wet with the mists and smitten by the lights,
The Dragon of the great Pendragonship
Blaze, making all the night a steam of fire.
And even then he turn'd ; and more and more
The moony vapour rolling round the King,
Who seem'd the phantom of a Giant in it,
Enwound him fold by fold, and made him gray
And grayer, till himself became as mist
Before her, moving ghostlike to his doom.

Then she stretch'd out her arms and cried aloud
' Oh Arthur !' there her voice brake suddenly,
Then—as a stream that spouting from a cliff
Fails in mid air, but gathering at the base
Re-makes itself, and flashes down the vale—
Went on in passionate utterance.
                                    ' Gone—my lord !
Gone thro' my sin to slay and to be slain !
And he forgave me, and I could not speak.
Farewell ? I should have answer'd his farewell.
His mercy choked me.   Gone, my lord the King,
My own true lord ! how dare I call him mine ?
The shadow of another cleaves to me,
And makes me one pollution : he, the King,

Call'd me polluted : shall I kill myself?
What help in that? I cannot kill my sin,
If soul be soul ; nor can I kill my shame ;
No, nor by living can I live it down.
The days will grow to weeks, the weeks to months,
The months will add themselves and make the years,
The years will roll into the centuries,
And mine will ever be a name of scorn.
I must not dwell on that defeat of fame.
Let the world be ; that is but of the world.
What else? what hope? I think there was a hope,
Except he mock'd me when he spake of hope ;
His hope he call'd it ; but he never mocks,
For mockery is the fume of little hearts.
And blessed be the King, who hath forgiven
My wickedness to him, and left me hope
That in mine own heart I can live down sin
And be his mate hereafter in the heavens
Before high God.   Ah great and gentle lord,
Who wast, as is the conscience of a saint
Among his warring senses, to thy knights—
To whom my false voluptuous pride, that took
Full easily all impressions from below,
Would not look up, or half-despised the height
To which I would not or I could not climb—
I thought I could not breathe in that fine air

That pure severity of perfect light—
I wanted warmth and colour which I found
In Lancelot—now I see thee what thou art,
Thou art the highest and most human too,
Not Lancelot, nor another.   Is there none
Will tell the King I love him tho' so late?
Now—ere he goes to the great Battle? none:
Myself must tell him in that purer life,
But now it were too daring.   Ah my God,
What might I not have made of thy fair world,
Had I but loved thy highest creature here?
It was my duty to have loved the highest:
It surely was my profit had I known:
It would have been my pleasure had I seen.
We needs must love the highest when we see it,
Not Lancelot, nor another.'
                              Here her hand
Grasp'd, made her vail her eyes: she look'd and saw
• The novice, weeping, suppliant, and said to her
'Yea, little maid, for am *I* not forgiven?'
Then glancing up beheld the holy nuns
All round her, weeping; and her heart was loosed
Within her, and she wept with these and said.

'Ye know me then, that wicked one, who broke
The vast design and purpose of the King.

O shut me round with narrowing nunnery-walls,
Meek maidens, from the voices crying "shame."
I must not scorn myself: he loves me still.
Let no one dream but that he loves me still.
So let me, if you do not shudder at me
Nor shun to call me sister, dwell with you;
Wear black and white, and be a nun like you;
Fast with your fasts, not feasting with your feasts;
Grieve with your griefs, not grieving at your joys,
But not rejoicing; mingle with your rites;
Pray and be pray'd for; lie before your shrines;
Do each low office of your holy house;
Walk your dim cloister, and distribute dole
To poor sick people, richer in his eyes
Who ransom'd us, and haler too than I;
And treat their loathsome hurts and heal mine own;
And so wear out in almsdeed and in prayer
The sombre close of that voluptuous day,
Which wrought the ruin of my lord the King.'

She said: they took her to themselves; and she
Still hoping, fearing ' is it yet too late?'
Dwelt with them, till in time their Abbess died.
Then she, for her good deeds and her pure life,
And for the power of ministration in her,
And likewise for the high rank she had borne,

Was chosen Abbess, there, an Abbess, lived
For three brief years, and there, an Abbess, past
To where beyond these voices there is peace.

DEDICATION.

OF THE "IDYLLS OF THE KING."

THESE to His Memory—since he held them dear,
Perchance as finding there unconsciously
Some image of himself—I dedicate,
I dedicate, I consecrate with tears—
These Idylls.

           And indeed He seems to me
Scarce other than my own ideal knight,
'Who reverenced his conscience as his king;
Whose glory was, redressing human wrong;
Who spake no slander, no, nor listened to it;
Who loved one only and who clave to her—'
Her—over all whose realms to their last isle,
Commingled with the gloom of imminent war,
The shadow of His loss drew like eclipse,

Darkening the world. We have lost him : he is gone :
We know him now : all narrow jealousies
Are silent ; and we see him as he moved,
How modest, kindly, all-accomplish'd, wise,
With what sublime repression of himself,
And in what limits, and how tenderly ;
Not swaying to this faction or to that ;
Not making his high place the lawless perch
Of wing'd ambitions, nor a vantage-ground
For pleasure ; but thro' all this tract of years
Wearing the white flower of a blameless life,
Before a thousand peering littlenesses,
In that fierce light which beats upon a throne,
And blackens every blot : for where is he
Who dares foreshadow for an only son
A lovelier life, a more unstain'd, than his?
Or how should England dreaming of *his* sons
Hope more for these than some inheritance
Of such a life, a heart, a mind as thine,
Thou noble Father of her Kings to be,
Laborious for her people and her poor—
Voice in the rich dawn of an ampler day—
Far-sighted summoner of War and Waste
To fruitful strifes and rivalries of peace—
Sweet nature gilded by the gracious gleam
Of letters, dear to Science, dear to Art,

Dear to thy land and ours, a Prince indeed,
Beyond all titles, and a household name,
Hereafter, thro' all times, Albert the Good.

  Break not, O woman's-heart, but still endure ;
Break not, for thou art Royal, but endure,
Remembering all the beauty of that star
Which shone so close beside Thee, that ye made
One light together, but has past and leaves
The Crown a lonely splendour.

                  May all love,
His love, unseen but felt, o'ershadow Thee,
The love of all Thy sons encompass Thee,
The love of all Thy daughters cherish Thee,
The love of all Thy people comfort Thee,
Till God's love set Thee at his side again !

BRADBURY AND EVANS, PRINTERS, WHITEFRIARS.